# Toils and Snares

An Alaskan Grace Christian Suspense Novel

Alana Terry

**Note: The views of the characters in this novel do not necessarily reflect the views of the author**, nor is their behavior necessarily condoned.



christianbooks.today

# CHAPTER 1

LAST NIGHT, I DREAMED I went back to the cabin. The wind rushed against my face as I rode my father's four-wheeler down the familiar wooded path. The summer sun shone through the trees. I breathed in the fresh air, trying to remember the last time I felt so at peace. So alive.

And then the cabin came into view, not the trash heap that exists today, but the charming cottage of my memory. Mom would cluck her tongue and tell me it was only for a few weeks, remind me that if I wanted to come home I could drive the four-wheeler to the lodge and call her to pick me up early. And I would laugh and tell her that as soon as summer was over I'd be back with her in Anchorage, with its traffic lights and its noise pollution and its depressing concrete sidewalks. I'd voluntarily return with her to that world where litter floated around empty parking lots, where Mom and I stressed together over the money that wasn't in the bank, where landlords could force you to move with only a month's notice, where Mom and I fantasized together of a better life without care or worry.

For three seasons of the year, I was her anxiety-ridden shoulder to cry on, a younger version of her care-worn self.

But not in summer. In summer, I wasn't the shy girl who alarmed her schoolteachers because I was skinny and malnourished. I was Snow White, spending my enchanted days outside with woodland creatures, cheerfully keeping house for not seven, but one mysterious forest dweller I adored more than life itself. There I spent the happiest days of my childhood, my fingers stained nearly black from the juice of the wild blueberries, my skin bronzed and freckled from the 24-hour sunlight that streamed in as I trudged behind my father, who hiked and fished and tracked black bears. There I learned the distinct sounds of the Alaskan wilderness, recognizing every bird call, knowing the time of day or night by the angle of the sun, breathing in fresh mountain air so pure that when I returned home ready to start another agonizingly tedious school year in Anchorage, I felt like the city air might suffocate me.

The cabin of my childhood no longer exists. I know that if I were to find my way down that overgrown path today, what waited for me at the end of the trail wouldn't be a tangible representation of all the happy magic of my youth. Instead of my summer home, there would be only rubble and ash. A pile of debris, a makeshift memorial, and memories I'm not strong enough to confront.

I'm no longer a girl, running carefree through the mountains. Now I'm a woman, my soul burdened with the crushing weight of all the truths I know ... truths I can never go back in time and change, no matter how hard I wish.

No matter how hard I pray.

# CHAPTER 2

"You were talking in your sleep again," my roommate tells me.

I try to wipe away the fogginess from my brain as I rub my aching temples. "Sorry," I respond. "What did I say?"

Becca shrugs. "The usual." She looks at me with so much sympathy and understanding that I wish I hadn't asked. I turn away, feeling ashamed and exposed.

"Anyway," Becca says, "I'm late. I've got to be at work in ten minutes or Danny will lose her mind."

I'm thankful that Becca knows me well enough to change the subject, and I glance at the clock. "You want me to start some coffee for you?"

"Nah," Becca answers as she flashes me that winsome smile that gets her so many great tips at Danny's Diner. "The way you make it, you'd put me into a sugar coma. I'll get my caffeine fix at work."

"Don't be so sure," I tease. "You won't have a single minute to yourself your entire shift."

Becca grins. "You miss the bustle, admit it. By the way, did I ever tell you that the guys at Table 20 still ask about you?"

I roll my eyes. "Only every single day."

I don't want to talk about the diner. I don't want to tell Becca that I actually miss working at Danny's. It would feel like a sort of betrayal, especially with as much time as we used to spend together complaining about the hard work and the more miserable customers we still had to serve with plastered-on smiles, degrading ourselves for the hope of a better tip, draining our energy for a dollar here, an extra percentage point there. Sometimes I feel like the most ungrateful woman in the state of Alaska.

Who but a masochist would actually miss working at a place like that?

A few minutes later, I'm sitting at the table, staring into a cup of steaming coffee when Becca steps into the kitchen. She tosses me a bridal magazine she picked up last week. "You chosen your design yet?"

I fidget with the ring on my finger, still unaccustomed to its feel, still not entirely convinced the last year hasn't been some sort of bizarre dream. Maybe James doesn't even exist. I've created some elaborate fantasy to cope with the horror show my life has felt like ever since my father's death, my mother's diagnosis. I'm a vivid enough daydreamer I wouldn't put it past me.

"Hello? This is Earth calling Daphne Winters. Come in, Daphne?"

I glance up at my roommate and blush. She's always catching me drifting off into my own world of thoughts. "What did you say?"

"I asked if you liked that Lily Beaumont empire gown I earmarked."

I look at *Modern Bride* and the multicolored Post-Its Becca has plastered on every other page. "Yeah," I answer even though I have no idea which specific gown she's referencing. "It was nice."

"Nice?" Becca's eyes widen. "Girl, if I were engaged to a Maxwell, I'd be channeling my inner Bridezilla and demanding that Lily Beaumont herself personally make me some kind of custom design." She grins mischievously. "What's the point of marrying into all that oil money if you don't plan on using at least some of it?"

Talk like this about my future in-laws makes me uneasy. Becca knows I'd be in love with James if he lived in a tent next to Ship Creek. The fact that his family is so well-known in Anchorage feels like a liability more often than an asset, especially given my past.

I let out a sigh. I don't want to admit it, even to myself, but I'm more nervous this morning than normal. Yesterday was the day our engagement announcement appeared in the paper, and I've been on edge ever since. I hate being the center of attention, and I'm terrified that someone will see it, someone from my hometown, someone who knows the hidden truths about my past and where I come from.

Becca slings her purse across her shoulder. "You have any big plans for the day?"

I keep staring into my coffee. "Mrs. Maxwell's stopping by this morning." I can't for the life of me remember if we're meeting with the wedding planner, interviewing caterers, going over guest lists, or something else entirely.

Becca's shaking her head at me, that look I know so well, the one that says, *You have no idea how good you've got it.* "Well, ask her if any of her fancy rich friends have any handsome, eligible sons and send them over to my section at Danny's. It's no fair that you get all the good luck."

I force a smile, but Becca's already turned her back and grabbed her keys. "All right, Starry Eyes, I've gotta run." She looks over her shoulder and flashes me one last dazzling grin. "Some of us plebes still have to work for a living, you know."

# CHAPTER 3

ONCE BECCA LEAVES, I refill my coffee and add enough sweetener to waken the dead, which in a way is exactly my aim. Seated on a folding chair at the card table Becca and I use as a dining room set, I let the steam from the mug rise to my face. It's still early, and I have hours stretching out ahead of me before Mrs. Maxwell and I are scheduled to meet. I get anxious every time I even think about James' mom, so I banish her from my mind and prepare my space.

I remove my roommate's dinner leftovers from the wobbly table, along with a few pieces of junk mail and Becca's gifted copy of *Modern Bride*. Now that I have room to work, I grab my backpack and spread out my supplies. Ever since I first heard of the idea of a prayer trigger, unpacking my bag has taken on almost ritualistic qualities. The individual items remind me to pray for something specific, and I've matched the first letters of each of my supplies to something on my prayer list.

As I take out my journal, I pray for James. The mnemonic is easy to remember, J for journal as well as my fiancé's first name. I figure with our different backgrounds and family histories, we need all the help we can get as we prepare to start our lives together, and so I hold my notebook in my hands and the love of my life in my heart.

Next comes out my sketch pad. The S reminds me to pray for the sisters of mercy who take care of my mom. It's not a religious nursing home, and her favorite caretaker, Gus, is a guy friend I've known since high school, but somehow the association was made and now it sticks.

The pens I pull out make me think of a pulpit, and so I pray over the church that James pastors. Technically, Anchorage Grace is my church home too, although after all this time attending, I still wonder when I'll start to actually feel like I belong. These thoughts signal dangerous territory, however, so I quickly pull out my Bible and open to the Song of Solomon.

Sometimes, Scripture journaling feels like one more thing to check off my list, nothing more than a somewhat unique way to have my quiet time with God before I jump into the busier parts of my schedule. But this morning, with hours of free time stretching out before me, I allow myself to daydream as I copy various verses, changing up the fonts and the colors with no obvious pattern or plan, trusting my creative instinct to make the final product something cohesive and complete by the time I'm done.

*I am my beloved's and my beloved is mine* ... It's still so hard for me to wrap my brain around the fact that I'm here, doodling in my prayer journal, asking God to bless my engagement and future marriage to James Maxwell. Not all that long ago, I wouldn't have dared to dream a love story like ours was even remotely possible. I think back to the first day we met last year. Becca and I were enjoying a much-appreciated lull between the breakfast and lunch crowds at Danny's when she grabbed me by the arm and eyed the man who just walked in the door. He was tall, confident, well-dressed, the exact type of customer my roommate loved to ogle.

"Flip a coin?" she asked, but I told Becca it was up to the hostess whose section he sat in. Sometimes she teases that she wishes she'd taken her chances with a coin toss. I know it's a joke, good-natured. Nothing at all like the rumor that later started circling Danny's, the speculation that James' mother secretly paid the hostess to seat her son in my section, as if someone like me needed to be handpicked by my future mother-in-law in order for a man like James to even notice me. I did my best to ignore the whispers, even though they did nothing to bolster my already shaky self-esteem.

"They're just jealous," Becca would always remind me. "God knows if I had the chance I'd love for someone rich and handsome to swoop in and rescue me from a life of waiting tables."

The irony was that in spite of how desperately Becca wanted to find true love, romance was the farthest thing on my mind when I met James last summer. My mom had recently moved into a nursing home. She was only in her fifties, but early-onset dementia had already been stripping away her identity for several years. I was still reeling from the guilt of abandoning her, suffocating under the grief, mentally and spiritually exhausted from watching our worst nightmares come true as she deteriorated before my eyes. I spent my days back then in such a stupor, I didn't even notice James return and become a regular in my section until Becca pointed it out.

And in case I ever wonder if miracles really do happen, one year later I'm here with my Bible journal, wearing the Maxwell family heirloom on my left hand.

*You are altogether beautiful, my darling.* My pens move as fast as my thoughts, first flitting to memories of the diner, of James' sweet nature and charm, the night he proposed, how happy we are together. My colors darken and my thoughts shift to my mother, the hymns she used to sing to me, the light shining in her eyes before snuffed out by disease, her brain, shriveled now both literally and figuratively, the day I drove her to the Pioneer Peaks Nursing Home and left her there, my heart splintering into pieces like shards of breaking ice.

I miss my mom even though I visit her every single day.

I miss her so much.

My cell phone beeps, and I glance at the incoming text. *Morning. Hope you slept well last night!*

I smile and type James a response, adding a cute little gif of two cartoon bunnies hugging under a heart. It's cheesy, but I want him to know how much I love him, how excited I am to be starting our lives together. If it was up to me, we'd have a simple wedding as soon as practically possible, but James' mom seems convinced that you need at least a year and a half to plan an appropriate ceremony. As soon as the engagement ring was on my finger, his family expected me to quit my job at Danny's Diner and spend my days as a full-time bride-to-be. The good news is I'm not bored. A flexible part-time job at the church, daily visits to my mom, and time spent with James and his family keep me plenty busy. So much has changed in this past year this gift of time could be seen as a blessing, at least when you look at it in a certain light.

I stare at my journal, trying to decide what else it needs. Next I plan to color something to hang on Mom's wall. She's lost the ability to read Bible verses, but I still try to do what I can to keep her room bright and cheerful. If I were living in that home, I'd want any extra splash of color I could get my hands on. The thought leaves me with that all-too familiar sense of guilt. Maybe now that I have more freedom in my schedule I should consider moving her in with me. I've ruminated over the idea almost every day, spent hours talking about it with Gus at the home, but as many times as I've examined the issue from every conceivable angle, the logistics don't add up. Mom gave up her lease when we moved her into Pioneer Peaks, and rent in Anchorage has become exorbitant since then. We'd never find something for the price she was paying. As for this place, I can't just kick Becca out, and even if I didn't have a roommate, this little third-story apartment isn't designed to accommodate an Alzheimer's patient with gait issues.

Once James and I get married, we could move Mom into the spare bedroom of the parsonage. Right now there's nothing in there but a bookshelf, an old rocking chair, and a doggy bed for his springer spaniel. In addition to his salary from the church, James still has a trust his grandparents set up as well as shares from when he used to work for his dad's oil company. I don't know all his financial details, but he's certainly well off enough that we could pay for a hospital bed and minor adjustments to make the log cabin more accessible.

But as hard as it is to admit, what my mother needs is a round-the-clock caretaker. All my love for her aside, she's simply too much for me to watch over by myself.

The thought makes me cringe, and the shame has poured itself onto my journal where I've doodled half a dozen looming spirals in dark blacks and blues and browns. No, that's not what I wanted. I flip to a blank page. Maybe it's not the right type of mood to be in Song of Solomon. When I'm bombarded with guilt and anxiety and every other negative emotion in the thesaurus, my usual portion of Scripture is Psalms, which is where I turn now, waiting for the right verse to catch my attention.

*Keep me safe, my God, for in you I take refuge.* Before I know what's happening, the words are on paper, scrawling teals and magentas that cover the entire sheet. My heart's racing with an almost indescribable excitement, a reckless abandon where I'm lost in my art, my prayers, my creation.

*Keep me safe, my God, for in you I take refuge.* The letters are done, but now the artistic maximalist in me won't stop until there's not a single white spot on the paper. I don't know if it's minutes that pass or hours, all I know is that when I'm done, I hardly remember the work I did at all. It's almost as if I'm looking at someone else's artwork for the very first time.

*Keep me safe, my God, for in you I take refuge.* The verse is calming, meant to give promises of hope and assurance. The rest of the page is a splash of colors and shapes and emotion. And then the abstract begins to coalesce in my field of vision. It's happened to me before so now I don't even bother to wonder at the process. While working, I'm adding colors and textures and shade in what feels like a random manner, but then after I look at the final piece, I often see images and meaning I never consciously chose to convey. That's what happens to me now, and I feel a heavy sinking in my heart.

*Keep me safe, my God, for in you I take refuge.*

Now the randomness of it all, even the placement of the letters like trees makes sense. I feel slightly queasy, but it's not just from the rush of creative adrenaline that's now draining out of my blood vessels, my energy spent. My phone beeps from an incoming message, and my hand is trembling just a little when I pick it up. Mrs. Maxwell texts as if she's writing an old-fashioned letter.

*Dear Daphne,*

*I'm sorry to say I was tied up this morning with urgent business so instead of picking you up myself, I'll send the car to collect you around 11 am. Looking forward to lunch.*

*Best, Beatrice*

I barely think about the note or the plans I have with James' mother or why she's sending her fancy driver over. Instead, I shut my eyes, hoping and praying that what I saw in the picture was wrong, my feverish imagination getting the best of me.

But when I dare to glance back at the page, it's even clearer this time. I know this place. I know these trees, that sloping trail, those woods, landmarks etched in my memory forever.

I've drawn my father's cabin, except it's not the safe enclosure I grew up in. Not the home of my happiest summers, my cherished memories.

It's the dilapidated shed where they found my father's body.

# CHAPTER 4

Beatrice Maxwell greets me at the front door of her condo against the coastline in downtown Anchorage.

"Daphne, you made it." There's a smile on her face but minimal emotion in her voice as she leans forward and gives me air kisses near both cheeks. "Come in. I'm sorry I couldn't pick you up myself, but I'm so glad you arrived on time."

She gives the driver a dismissive tilt of the head, and he pulls out of her driveway.

I've been in Mrs. Maxwell's condo plenty of times, but as often as I try, I'm never fully prepared for her entryway, whose vaulted ceiling reaches up the entire three stories of their home. There's a crystal chandelier hanging high above us, a chandelier I know is cleaned on a regular basis by the house staff using an extension ladder.

While I'm working hard not to stare above our heads, Mrs. Maxwell glances at me. "Oh, sweetie, I didn't know you'd been to see your mother this morning. Here, let's go up to my closet and find you something to wear. No reason to sit around all afternoon with a bunch of stuffy old women while you're in your street clothes."

My face flushes, but I refuse to glance down at the leggings and fitted blouse I took so long trying to choose. It's moments like these I can't help but compare myself to James' ex-fiancé. It's been several years since his very public breakup with the senator's daughter, but it seems like whenever I'm with Mrs. Maxwell I feel even more keenly how different I am from women like Manderley Danvers, the tall and gracious and upper-class socialite. The type of woman James was expected to marry.

I slip off my shoes and follow Mrs. Maxwell up both flights of stairs. When we reach the top, she stops the household manager, who's cleaning the en suite bathroom. "Phillipa, our company will be here in just a few minutes. Could you go and see if the caterer needs any help in the kitchen?" Phillipa has always struck me as someone I'd love to get to know better, but before I can catch her eye or give her a friendly smile, she's silently bustled out of the room, leaving Mrs. Maxwell and me alone on the spacious third floor, which consists entirely of the main bedroom, bathroom, and two walk-in closets.

Mrs. Maxwell is prattling on about everybody she's expecting over for lunch. I don't recognize the names, but that doesn't mean I haven't met them before. Some people are great at remembering names, others at faces. It seems as though I lack talent in both.

"I thought we were meeting Elle today." I think back to the texts Mrs. Maxwell and I have exchanged, trying to remember if a lunch date with her friends jogs anything in my mind. Sometimes I'm scared that if I'm not careful, I'll become like my mother, forgetful, confused, a shadow of the woman I've always been, the woman I hope to remain.

I quickly force the thought out of my head.

"Elle?" Mrs. Maxwell repeats, as if the name is distasteful to her. "The wedding planner? That's Friday, darling."

"Oh. I must have gotten my days confused."

Mrs. Maxwell eyes me with a smile. I wonder if she's thinking about my mother, too, trying to decide if she wants to resume her attempts to force her son to convince me to get one of those genetic tests that will tell me if my brain will also one day become a mound of holes and decay. I've told James I don't want to know, I'm not ready for that type of knowledge yet. What I haven't told him is that if the tests show I have dementia in my future, I have no doubt his mother would do her best to keep us from marrying and ruining the family's good name.

So instead I wake up each day choking down a fear that I refuse to acknowledge. When James and I walk through the parsonage, talking about the changes we'll make when we're married, I don't mention that I'm glad it doesn't have any stairs I could fall down if I inherit my mother's unsteady gait. When he talks to me about future kids, I plaster on a smile and beg my face not to betray the fact that I'm wondering if in a couple decades I'll forget these hypothetical children I raised.

I know that if it came down to it, I could trust James to look after me. He wouldn't be the type to toss me into a nursing home like a discarded pair of boots or rusty toilet bowl that started leaking. James is infinitely patient, infinitely kind. It's one of the thousands of things I love about him. Every day, I thank God that a man like him wants to spend the rest of his life with a woman like me, hard as it is for me to understand or accept.

I'm ruminating about my future with James, hopefully a future that doesn't involve my brain getting riddled with the plaques and tangles that the doctors always tell me about when I take my mom in for her appointments. Then I'm whisked back to the present when Mrs. Maxwell flings open the French doors that lead to the smaller of her walk-in closets, and she's back to business.

"Let's see," she muses, fingering the colorful blouses and sweaters on the bottom rail. "Before she left for law school, Jillian sorted out some old things she didn't wear anymore. Let's just see if anything here fits you." She pulls out a few of her daughter's tops, most still with tags on them, and frowns as she considers each. Finally, she chooses something silky and lavender. "We can make this work. Here, put this on. If we had the time we could probably also find you some pants, but I suppose what you've got on will have to do. I've got to go downstairs. I'll meet you in the kitchen when you're dressed. See you in a few."

She leans in for a parting air kiss, a ritual I'm not sure I'll ever get used to no matter how long James and I are married. She floats past, leaving an aromatic trail of perfume and shampoo and body wash in her wake, and I look at the light purple tunic she handed me. I haven't met James' sister yet, but I have to admit I like her fashion style. The fabric seems to shimmer in the soft light. Wearing it feels like being wrapped up in the wings of a thousand butterflies, and I take a moment to examine myself in the mirror, trying to imagine what life would feel like if I were James's sister, if clothes like this were so common I couldn't even pack them all when I moved out east to attend law school.

I think about what it might feel like to be the mistress of this home, talking to Phillipa every morning, telling her what part of the house to have cleaned, what types of flowers I wanted in the entryways and by my bedside. We'd talk regularly, Phillipa and me, and not just about the housework. We'd become such good friends that sometimes I'd invite her to keep me company in the evenings, and we'd stay up late watching romcoms in the oversized loveseat while the fire roared gently beside us.

I imagine coming into this closet one morning, and while Phillipa's making the bed or changing the sheets, I'd pick out a dress and exclaim, "Phillipa, this looks like it'll fit you, and I think you'd look lovely wearing it to church on Sunday." And she'd tell me she couldn't possibly, but I'd assure her that she simply must, and we'd have a giggle, as if we'd dared each other to do something illegal like shoplift.

My daydream is interrupted by the sound of the doorbell announcing the arrival of the first of the lunch guests. I remember that I'm supposed to already be in the kitchen, and I toss one last glance at myself in the mirror before heading down to meet Beatrice Maxwell's gaggle of friends.

# CHAPTER 5

"WELL, DAPHNE," ONE OF my new lunchmates announces after the salad plates are cleared, "it certainly is nice to finally spend some time getting to know you."

Her comment is met with murmurs of agreement.

"So nice to share a meal together," another responds. "I've seen you at church, you know, but I never had the chance to come up and say hi until now."

"It's a large church," one woman declares.

"Yes," says another, "such a large congregation for such a young pastor."

Mrs. Maxwell is sitting high in her chair at the head of the table. "Of course, James has proven himself capable in the worlds of business and finance. It's no surprise he can manage a large congregation as adeptly as he does."

"Of course," the guests around the table demurely agree.

There's a slightly awkward silence until the woman to my right, a somewhat nasally-sounding Mrs. van Hopper, grabs my forearm and exclaims, "Well, Daphne, I just loved that photo of you two in the paper. A most beautiful bride-to-be. I told my husband you were literally glowing."

This comment is met with several similar murmurs of agreement, albeit none nearly so enthusiastic, and I get the feeling Mrs. van Hopper's exaggerated gushing was more for the purpose of changing the subject than offering a genuine compliment. Truth be told, I still have no idea what James ever saw in a shy, freckled waitress like me.

"Daphne. Hmm ..." Mrs. van Hopper interjects. She seems as though she's the type of woman who couldn't stand any degree of silence without risking apoplexy. She leans toward me, in spite of how close we're already seated to one another. Her posture suggests she wants to have an intimate conversation, just the two of us, but her voice is loud enough I'm sure the Maxwell driver can hear it from across town or wherever he might be. "That's an interesting name. What does it mean?"

I've always hated talking about myself, especially if it might lead to stories from my past. That feeling is heightened now as I sit amongst this group of women I hardly know, women with whom I have almost nothing in common. My voice sounds timid and shy, even to myself, when I answer that my name means laurel tree. Since so many of these women attend my fiancé's church, I don't mention that Daphne was a nymph from Greek mythology, assuming they might find it a bit too heathen of a namesake. Instead, I simply add, "It was my grandmother's name," and heads around the table nod. Apparently, my answer has satiated their curiosity.

"A lovely name for a lovely young woman." Mrs. van Hopper turns to the women around the table and speaks even louder now, a feat I didn't imagine possible just moments earlier. "I remember meeting Daphne the very first weekend she started attending Anchorage Grace." She tilts her chin up as if this confession gives her a certain degree of distinction, a certain type of insider knowledge. She looks at the woman across from her. "You remember what I said, don't you? I said she certainly is a pretty little thing, and not at all what I was expecting. She's so different, you know, from Manderley."

I suck in my breath as if this loud, somewhat dowdy woman has punched me in the stomach. When I dare to raise my gaze, I see several mouths around the table gaping open, as if the group has simultaneously sucked in all the oxygen in the house at the mention of James' ex-fiancée.

"Well, it's true," Mrs. van Hopper declares rather defiantly. "Manderley's so tall and graceful and has that long black hair ..."

I toss a desperate glance to James' mom.

"An important reminder that looks aren't everything." Mrs. Maxwell straightens her spine and glares at her guest before offering me a smile that feels like the warmest gesture I've ever received from anybody. "In fact, we're thrilled that Daphne and James have found each other. Such a blessing from the Lord."

Relief settles over the table. The collective sigh of relief that follows is so potent that I can almost taste the sardine paste from the Ceasar dressing in the air around us. I shift uncomfortably in my seat, my hands clammy, and wonder what in the world I can say to keep the conversation away from the perfectly manicured and pedigreed senator's daughter that James was meant to have married. Aware that everyone is trying hard to pretend they aren't staring at me, I take a bite of my oversized croissant. If only it were large enough I could hide my entire blushing face behind it.

"Well now," exclaims one of the younger guests, a woman who's probably not more than ten years my senior. I forget her name, and I think this is the first time she's spoken during the entire meal. "How are the wedding plans coming? Have you set a date?"

My mouth is still full of buttery, flaky dough, so Mrs. Maxwell answers for me. "We meet with Elle tomorrow." As Alaska's one and only celebrity wedding planner, Elle needs no last name to be recognized by everyone seated here. In fact, I'm not even certain I've ever known what her last name actually is.

"What about the dress?" Mrs. van Hopper inserts, grabbing my forearm. "What designer will you be going with?"

I still haven't gotten used to how everyone, including my own roommate, thinks that my entire life's purpose for the next year and a half is to make concrete plans for my wedding. The Maxwells even gave the church a special donation so they could hire me to work in their office. It's a part-time, very flexible position, but the stipend is the same pay I got during my busiest weeks at the diner. The secretarial position is meant to give me time to devote to preparing a ceremony worthy of the Maxwells' status and budget. Still, I feel as if I have hardly anything to show for all that extra time and my future in-laws' generosity except for Becca's copy of *Modern Bride.*

Thinking of the magazine sparks a memory, and I'm thankful to have something to contribute to the conversation. "I've been looking at some dresses from Lily Beaumont."

The younger woman almost chokes on her sparkling water. Heads turn to Mrs. Maxwell or to their plates or to the large bay window and its view of Cook Inlet, bathed in midday summer sun. Nobody looks at me, even though I have no idea what I've done wrong. Did I mispronounce the designer's name? Now that I think about it, the only time I've heard it spoken out loud rather than just seen it in print is when my roommate mentions what dress she wants me to wear. My face flushes hot, and when I toss a questioning glance toward Mrs. Maxwell, she's looking over her shoulder as if something in the kitchen has absorbed a hundred percent of her attention.

"Lily Beaumont has some nice options," one guest finally contributes meekly, breaking the strange spell and prompting a few other women to nod in agreement.

"I think I heard something about her summer line in Target," another adds. "Nice clothes. Kind of sweet and unpretentious," she finishes, clearing her throat.

"Well," exclaims Mrs. van Hopper, "before you go for all your fittings and whatnot, you come make an appointment to see my hubby. He works out of the Lake Otis medical center and just does a wonderful job with the girls."

"Girls?" I glance around the table, hoping for subtle clues to help me decipher her meaning.

Mrs. van Hopper grins as if she and I are privy to some massive secret, and she playfully shimmies her shoulders. "You know. The ladies."

"Dr. van Hopper is a plastic surgeon," Mrs. Maxwell states dryly, dabbing the corners of her mouth with a cloth napkin and looking slightly displeased.

I'm still confused until Mrs. van Hopper leans closer. "Boob jobs, darling," she whispers so loudly that I'm certain even Phillipa in the other room can hear her. I want to sink into my chair and die.

"Not everybody gets work done before their wedding," someone states, and I bless them for coming to my rescue.

"No, of course not," Mrs. van Hopper answers defensively. "I got mine after I weaned my daughter."

"Mine were a graduation gift," another chimes in. "College," she hurriedly adds. "Not high school."

"I'm not sure at all if Daphne's into that sort of procedure," Mrs. Maxwell declares, offering what I choose to interpret as a conversational life saver.

"Of course," women chirp, and "certainly not for everyone," and "might be strange for a pastor's wife."

Mrs. Maxwell clears her throat. "Some of you might not know this yet, but Daphne's mother was a very gifted artist. In fact, you can even see one of her paintings at the Ted Stevens airport."

Mrs. van Hopper lets out an exaggerated gasp. "Did she make that beautiful landscape by baggage claim with that lovely fireweed?"

"No," I stammer, "but um, she has a small portrait of an Athabascan elder in the upstairs waiting area."

"Ah." There's no further comment. For a second I hope nobody asks any further questions about my mother, and then I'm immediately ashamed of my wish.

"Do you do any painting, Daphne?"

"A little," I admit.

"Daphne is very talented," Mrs. Maxwell adds, and I hope I'm not so desperate for her approval that I'm making up the hint of pride detected in her voice.

Mrs. van Hopper squeezes my arm tightly. "Do you do pet portraits, darling? I want to get a painting of my little June bug to hang by the fireplace where he loved to doze. I have a photo you could work from, of course. We'd use one before he had his eye removed, obviously, or maybe you could just put in a second eye where his slit was. I like to remember him when he was happy, bless his little bichon heart. Poor little baby was just too sweet for this world."

I'm spared the embarrassment of having to respond when Phillipa enters to serve the next course.. Maybe the ladies sense my discomfort, or maybe they're bored with me, or maybe Mrs. Maxwell deliberately steers the conversation in different directions, but it's not until the dessert plates are cleared away and we're drinking tea and coffee in the living room when the general attention returns to me.

"So, Daphne," someone exclaims. "You have to tell us all how you met James. I don't think I know the story at all."

I shoot a quick glance at Mrs. Maxwell. I would love for her to jump in and answer this question for me, but she's whispering something to Phillipa who's filling coffee mugs and pouring tea. A dozen women are staring at me expectantly.

"We met at Danny's Diner." I hope this will be enough, but the questions and the comments pile on.

*How interesting.*

*Is that where the men's prayer breakfast meets?*

*I love their cinnamon rolls.*

Mrs. van Hopper folds her arms across her ample chest. "How do you even strike up a conversation with someone at a diner, is what I want to know," she exclaims. Even though we aren't sitting side by side anymore, her voice still grates my ears, but at least she isn't grabbing my arm every other word. She lets out a chuckle, glancing around the circle for support. "I mean, I can't imagine that he just walked over to your table and interrupted your breakfast and introduced himself? No respectful young man would be so brazen."

I lower my gaze. The truth was bound to come out eventually. I just wish it weren't accompanied by this hot flash of shame. "He was a regular in my section." I wince as the words come out, but when I dare glance up, nobody seems to understand. I realize my diner vocabulary is as foreign here as it would be to me if the guests had started spouting off words and statistics about trust funds or charitable grants.

I tilt my chin confidently in a gesture I've seen James' mother perfect and tell them, "I was a waitress. I met James when I was serving his table."

The room goes quiet. Phillipa is standing in the entryway to the kitchen, and I catch her looking at me sympathetically. Her expression is one of compassion, but before I can offer her a smile of thanks, she hurries out of the room. Mrs. Maxwell, stands up with deliberate grace, comes to my side, and forces my sweaty hand into hers. She stands defiantly beside me, as if daring anybody to speak against me or my previous profession. I feel strength in her words when she tells her guests, "Daphne is an answer to prayer and just what James needs."

I feel a flood of gratitude toward my future mother-in-law even as my face continues to flush. One day I hope to find a way to show her how much her words mean to me.

"You're marrying at Anchorage Grace, I assume?" This question from Mrs. van Hopper shifts the room's equilibrium back to baseline, and several other women toss out their comments and suggestions about weddings, restoring a more casual feel to the conversation.

"I was invited to a bridal shower for my husband's step-niece, and they held it at the Russian Tea Garden. It was delightful. Absolutely delightful."

"If you're looking for a florist, I'll find out who did my neighbor's. It was a winter wedding, reds and maroons and God bless them not a single poinsettia in sight!"

I entertain recommendations for cake designers, caterers, even a bagpipe band. At some point I'm given the name of an acquaintance of an acquaintance, an esthetician specializing in freckle removal. It's a service I had no idea even existed and one which I would have died to afford back in my insecure teen days. Then the conversation naturally shifts and meanders like a slow-moving river. One moment they're discussing hot flashes and the next gossiping about a worship leader from a church in midtown.

While the ladies chat, I let my mind roam naturally, changing just as often and with the same ease as their topics of discussion. One minute I'm wondering if laser freckle removal is painful, the next about how back in high school my friend Gus told me he liked my freckles because they made me look friendly. Then just as unexpectedly, I'm decorating the parsonage living room in my mind or wondering if the artists who compete in the ice sculpting competition in Fairbanks feel depressed when the weather warms up, destroying all evidence of their craft.

Finally, Mrs. Maxwell glances toward the dining room. Phillipa appears not a second later. "Phillipa, it's just about time to show our guests where their bags have been kept." I glance at the clock, surprised that it's still so early in the day. I would have guessed it must already be close to dinnertime.

After the usual exchange of pleasantries and some invasive hugs from women whose names I've already forgotten, the house is quiet. For a terrible moment, I'm afraid James' mom will want to talk to me about the luncheon, about what I did wrong or forgot to do right. Instead, she simply leads me up to the third floor so I can change back into what she calls my street clothes.

"I hope you enjoyed yourself well enough. Sometimes these get-togethers can be a bit of a bore, I'll admit."

I feel as though Mrs. Maxwell's taking me into her confidence in a way she's never done before, and I don't know what to say.

"Thanks for everything," I finally manage to utter. "It really was nice getting to know more of the women from Anchorage Grace."

Mrs. Maxwell pauses at the closet door, turns around and looks at me. I want to find a way to tell her that I appreciate her support. I want to tell her that I understand her son and I are an unconventional match, but I'd never do anything to intentionally embarrass her, and I hope I live up to all her expectations for James. But before I can form these thoughts into words, she sucks in her breath and tilts up her chin. "You and James are coming to dinner tonight, right?"

Are we? I'm having such a hard time keeping everything straight in my head. I'm going to have to find an app that will send me constant reminders throughout the day of everything on my schedule. Then again, for that to be effective I'd have to remember to actually mark down all my appointments in my phone. Maybe one day I'll be like Mrs. Maxwell and have a household manager to oversee my calendar for me. Funny, but when I waited tables at Danny's I always remembered what shift I was on, even during those hectic times when it changed from day to day as drastically and as unpredictably as the weather in Anchorage.

"Dinner's at 7:30," Mrs. Maxwell says, "but it might be best if the two of you get here a little early." She holds my gaze in hers. "There's something I've been meaning to discuss with you both," she adds with an air of mysterious importance.

I try not to let my anxiety show on my face. I feel like I'm a kid again and my teacher just told me I have a meeting in the principal's office after school. Only instead of leaving class and finding out right then what kind of trouble I'm in, I have to act normal the rest of the day while all the while letting my imagination run wild with all the possible worst-case scenarios.

By the look in her eyes, I think Mrs. Maxwell's going to say something else, but then she seems to change her mind and pulls her heavy gaze away from me.

"You can leave that blouse on the bed, and I'll have Phillipa take it to the dry cleaner's." She gives me a once-over and frowns. “Actually, you better keep it. And since you’re here, why don’t you see if any of Jillian’s other things fit you. Phillipa can show you which section of the closet I’m talking about. I have a symphony league meeting to rush off to, I’m afraid, so I’ll say my goodbye here. I’ll send Phillipa up here to help you sort the closet. Just tell her when you’ve picked out everything you want, and she’ll have the driver take you home.”

# CHAPTER 6

I STARE AT THE clothes in Mrs. Maxwell's closet, waiting for Phillipa to join me before I take anything off its rack. In a way, isn't it just about any girl's dream to be given free rein to an entire wardrobe full of fashionable clothes? *Here, take what you want. Jillian doesn't have any use for it. Do you like this coat? It's from last winter's line, but at least it's still warm. Need a formal dress for the charity dinner? Sure, what color?*

Before my lunch with Mrs. Maxwell and her friends, I had lost myself in daydreams about stepping into this closet every single day. Phillipa would ask what I wanted to wear, and I'd say something like, "Oh, I'm not sure. I'm not going out at all today, so why don't you just hand me one of those kaftans. Maybe find me one that matches the new flower arrangement downstairs, not the one in the entryway, the one in the dining room." But now, I'm simply not in the mood. I can't pinpoint exactly what's wrong with me, but I'm tired and on edge. The lunch wasn't a horrific disaster like it could have been. I didn't spill soup on Mrs. van Hopper's lap or burp in public or accidentally divulge certain details about my dad. Part of me is glad that Mom was already slipping away when the entire truth came out. She never fully grasped it. Never fully understood. That much is a blessing, at least. But it also means I don't have anybody to talk to. Becca was the first person I ever told. And James knows too, of course, but my fiancé actually believed me when I told him this was all in the past.

"Daphne? Are you up here?"

I jump. "Oh, Phillipa, you startled me."

"I'm sorry. Mrs. Maxwell asked me to show you some of Jillian's things?"

"Yeah, I'm ... She ..." I can't figure out why I'm so flustered, why I feel as guilty as if Phillipa just caught me shoplifting.

She takes a gentle step past me into the closet. "Back here. Mrs. Maxwell says anything in this section that fits is yours if you want it. Once you find what you like, just hang them on this hook, and I'll start packing them. Mrs. Maxwell has some old garment bags you can use."

"Thanks, Phillipa." For the first time today, I manage to catch her eye for more than a split second. Her friendly expression gives me an idea. "Hey, we're both about the same size, and this is obviously more clothes than I could ever use. Do you want to pick some stuff out too? If Jillian isn't going to use any of it ..." My voice trails off, and I wonder if what I meant to be a generous offer is actually insulting. Here I am, taking discarded hand-me-downs from an oil heiress, and I'm offering the leftovers from what I don't want to the maid. I've become a giver of third-hand gifts, and I blush at my brazenness. In a few more years will I be even more like Mrs. Maxwell and her friends, even more out of touch with the 99%?

I think back to last December when I was still working full-time at Danny's and exhausted from the holiday rush. I waited on a table of middle-aged matrons, women who would have looked quite comfortable in Mrs. Maxwell's living room this afternoon. After I handed them their bill, they told me to wait, then they all took out their cell phones and began to film the entire interaction. They made such a show of it that I felt the eyes of nearly every patron and half of the staff on me.

"Before we call it a night," began the loudest one, a woman who might easily pass as Mrs. van Hopper's sister. She aimed her camera right at me. "Can you tell us your name and how old you are?"

I was too stunned to do anything but answer.

"Well, Daphne," she went on, "we are about to make your Christmas one you're never going to forget." She pulled a thick red envelope out from her designer purse. "One hundred dollar bills from each of us." She gestured to the smiling faces around the table, women whose expressions made them look like they were watching YouTube videos of baby elephants taking their first clumsy steps or bear cubs playing in a kiddie pool at the zoo.

"That will cover our meal," she declared loudly, "and the rest is all for you."

The women around the table clapped, as if I'd just put on some puppet show or song-and-dance routine for their personal enjoyment.

"Oh, look at the little lamb!" one of the women exclaimed. "We've made her entirely speechless!"

"Now, you take that home and give your kids the Christmas of their dreams!"

"It's not easy being a single mom in this economy."

I shoot a quick glance at my diner uniform, wondering what in the world would have given them the impression I have children.

"No need to thank us, sweetheart. We're just glad we could pass these blessings on to someone in need this year."

I know that somewhere the video clip still floats around online, and secretly I'm terrified of next holiday season when it might make its rounds again as a heartwarming display of human generosity. Of course, I split the money with both the front and back of the house. What I had left at the end bought me three-quarters of a tankful of gas. The shame and heat from that very public interaction scalds me to my core even now, and I'm mortified that I just put Phillipa in a similar situation. Unfortunately, I can't take back what I've said, and apologizing for my faux pas might make her even more uncomfortable.

I'm too appalled at my behavior to do anything but stare at my feet.

"I probably shouldn't," she says, but her eyes are kind and smiling. "Thank you for the offer, though. That was very kind."

There's an awkward silence. "Did you have a nice lunch?" Phillipa finally asks. I wonder if she's detected my discomfort, if that's why she offers me this olive branch in the form of small talk. Or maybe it's just because this is the first time the two of us have ever been able to speak alone, free from the watchful eyes of Mrs. Maxwell, my fiancé's mother and her boss. On the one hand, I feel that Phillipa and I could be kindred spirits, similar in age and in the disparity of our social backgrounds compared to the Maxwells. On the other hand, I'm marrying into the family that employs her, whereas she knows more about acceptable social behavior in Mrs. Maxwell's circle than I fear I ever will.

Even though my guess is that she's just being polite, I'm thankful for someone to talk to, eager to cleanse my social palette from the likes of Mrs. van Hopper and other ladies seated around the Maxwell dining room table. "It's a little intimidating, you know, meeting so many new people all at once." Now that I'm talking, I find it more difficult than it should be to stop. "I mean, they're just meeting one new person and have one new name to remember, but I'm meeting a dozen."

Phillipa nods. "You wouldn't enjoy my family get-togethers back home," she states.

I jump on this chance to learn about her background and ask where she's from. While we go through Mrs. Maxwell's closet, looking at clothes with price tags touting the equivalent of two weeks' worth of pay at the diner, Phillipa tells me about her large extended family in the Philippines, the aunts and uncles and cousins who make up their holiday gatherings.

"You must miss them so much," I say.

She shrugs. "I like my job."

It's an unwanted reminder that Phillipa is here with me because Mrs. Maxwell pays for her time. In a way, it's no different than what I did at the diner to cover my rent or what any employee does to keep their boss happy, but there's something about it that still leaves me unsettled.

"Do you have any family in the States?" I ask, and she tells me about a cousin in Florida.

"She's married to a doctor who's twice her age. He's not a kind man, but the money she sends back home has put all four of her sisters through school." Her gaze settles as if on something far in the distance, and she adds in a quiet voice, as if to herself, "Sometimes if I'm having a bad day, I tell myself that at least I'm not in her situation. If I'm sick of my work, I have a room over the garage and privacy at the end of the day. But even when my cousin's sick of her husband, she still has to sleep in the same bed as him night after night."

Phillipa sucks in her breath. A horrified expression comes across her face, a look of both embarrassment as well as surprise. I wonder if she forgot she was speaking out loud. I try to find some way to clear the tension in the air, to make her feel like I understand her. But I don't know what to say, and my face flushes hotter than a burnt coffee carafe at Danny's.

I stare at the clothes in the closet until my brain comes up with something to say to change the subject. "You know, I was just thinking. It might not feel right to take any of the clothes for yourself, but what about a small gift for your mom or your sisters or something? Maybe a couple of these scarves?" There are at least two dozen on a special hanger, all in vibrant shades of orange and yellow and lime green and all the bright, maxed-out colors I'd never wear. I take down two and thrust them into her hand. "Please," I beg. "I insist."

Phillipa isn't looking at the silky fabrics. Instead, she turns on her heel and says, "I better let the driver know you're ready to leave."

# CHAPTER 7

THE CHAUFFEUR DROPS ME off at the Kaladi Brothers Coffee Shop near the nursing home. A hot, sugary drink is exactly what I need before I go visit Mom. Worried I've insulted Phillipa, I've been texting with James, who thinks it's hilarious I offered his sister's clothes to the family household employee.

*Trust me*, he writes, *Phillipa is well compensated for her work. She doesn't need charity.*

I know it doesn't matter to James, but his words sting. I've spent so much mental energy around his family trying to say the right things, act the right way, wear the right clothes. It's exhausting.

*Just be yourself, and they'll come to love you as much as I do.* James tells me this all the time, the words of a privileged youngest son whose family is convinced he can do no possible wrong. James has been brought up in this world. He knows what kind of conversation is and isn't appropriate to have with the house staff. He knows how to laugh off busybody gossips like Mrs. van Hopper and never pays the least bit of attention to their opinion of him.

As I wait in line for a coffee and quick snack, I let my mind wander, picturing how different things would be right *now* if I were someone else, if I'd been brought up in James' social circle from birth. I imagine my life, my engagement, my relationship with James as if I were Manderley Danvers. Beautiful, luscious black hair. An enviable figure that perhaps had seen the sharp end of Dr. van Hopper's scalpel. A perfect political bloodline dating back to the earliest days of Alaska's statehood. If I were Manderley, I could stand tall beside Mrs. Maxwell, joking with enviable ease, always knowing exactly when to make eye contact, when to comfortably glance away so as not to seem either too forward or too insecure.

*A photograph, miss?* a man from the magazines would ask, small-scale paparazzi sent to cover this hypothetical engagement party the Maxwells and my family are throwing for James and me. I'd be wearing the exact right dress, nothing so gaudy it would make people talk, but perfectly formal and feminine. The best part of being Manderley is that I'd have no doubts, none at all. I'd believe just as firmly as I believed in the Alaska Pipeline that I had a right to be here, that I had a right to look this stunning in this fancy of a dress, that of course my parents and future in-laws would spare no expense throwing this lavish engagement party for me. I'd smile the dazzling smile of a strong, beautiful, confident woman, a woman who isn't full of herself but who also would never waste energy trying to pretend she was something less than she actually was.

Because if I was Manderley Danvers, I wouldn't have to pretend. I'd laugh and chink glasses with all the guests. The Mrs. van Hoppers would sidle up to me. We'd exchange a few words that would cost me absolutely no emotional energy, forgotten as soon as the pleasantries leave my mouth. Forgotten by me, but not by others.

*Don't you think she's charming?* the Mrs. van Hoppers would exclaim. *So elegant, so intelligent. Did you see how kind she is to the staff too? There's nothing at all pretentious about her. Where in the world did James ever find someone so beautiful and well-brought-up and so down-to-earth all in the same woman? She truly is extraordinary, isn't she?*

"Excuse me, miss." My daydream is interrupted by a lanky man in a Fairbanks hoodie who's standing behind me. "Sorry," he says, offering a conciliatory smile. "I was just trying to place where I know you from. Do you go to Anchorage Grace Church by any chance?"

For the briefest second, I'm embarrassed that this stranger caught me fantasizing. Then I remind myself that of course he has no idea what nonsense is passing through my mind as we wait in line for caffeine.

I return his smile. "Yeah. I've been going there a little less than a year."

"I thought you looked familiar." He holds out his hand. "You're engaged to Pastor James, right?"

I nod, flushing slightly as his glance darts down to my ring finger.

"That's me."

"I'm so sorry," he says. "I've forgotten your name."

I tell him, and he introduces himself as Clark. He's from a small town off the Glenn Highway called Tolsona, always wanted to move to the city, and has a job now working for *Anchorage Daily News*. By the time we near the front of the line, I'm surprised I don't know his social security number and his mother's maiden name as well.

"Wait a minute." He interrupts himself while he's telling me about the difference between Kaladi Brothers Coffee, an Alaskan staple, and Starbucks. "Have you lived in Anchorage your whole life? Because I swear you look like someone I knew back in Tolsona."

"I spent some summers near Eureka." The two towns are fifty miles apart, but in Alaskan terms, that makes us next-door neighbors.

"Oh yeah? Your family have land out that way? Wait a minute. I knew I recognized you. Aren't you Benji Chilkoot's cousin? I used to play hockey with him in middle school." Clark laughs. "Look at that. Small world, right? How is Benji? Last I heard he was in the Lower 48 on a hockey scholarship."

"Yeah," I answer. If he knows who my cousin is, then he knows who my father is too, hard as I've tried to run away from that part of my past. "Benji's good," I tell him, surprised at how small my voice sounds even in my own ears. "He's playing for the University of Michigan."

I glance imploringly toward the barista. I don't care about manners. I need to find a way to stop Clark from saying one more word.

The woman in front of me signs her receipt, and I hurry up to the counter, my lungs constricting in my chest. I'm about to spill out my order when Clark takes my arm. "Hey, I'm um ..." He stares at my feet. "I'm sorry about your dad. Frank, right? Frank Chilkoot?"

"Yeah, that's him. I'm sorry, I've got to ... um ..."

I turn and face the counter. I don't hear what he says next. I don't know if he continues peppering me with questions that I completely ignore or if he senses my discomfort and leaves me to fester in my own fear and anxiety and panic by myself. I hope God might open up a sinkhole right now and allow the earth to swallow me whole. I don't know if this stranger from my past says anything else to me or if he's completely oblivious to how terrified he's made me. All I know is I can't stay here.

"I said, are you ready to order?" the barista exclaims, annoyance edging into her voice.

"Sorry." I mumble something about leaving my wallet at home, rush out of the coffee shop, and refuse to look back.

# CHAPTER 8

I'M CALMER BY THE time the Pioneer Peaks Nursing Home comes into view. Some of that is thanks to the summer weather, low sixties, slight breeze, not a cloud in the sky. The dragonflies have just hatched, and as I walk past Goose Lake toward the nursing home, they dance in spirals around my face.

I called James on the walk. We usually find time to exchange a few words during the day, something more than texts. I didn't tell him about Clark. It's nothing, really. For all its vast wilderness, rural Alaska is like one big small town, and you don't live in any village or community along the Glenn without knowing who Frank Chilkoot is and what he did. Thankfully, the few locals like Clark from the coffee shop who remember Frank Chilkoot are few and far between. Hardly worth my time. Since he hated the idea of any type of government registry, he's not listed on my birth certificate. I have my mother's last name, and next year I won't even be Daphne Winters anymore. Instead I'll be Daphne Maxwell. I try to decide if it sounds sophisticated or not. I like to think it's somewhat distinguished, the name of someone interesting or important. But maybe it's just weird.

Instead of focusing any more of my mental energy on my father or on brazen strangers accosting me in line at a Kaladi Brothers, I think about how happy I'll be when I'm finally Daphne Maxwell. I imagine the sound of the pastor's voice as he announces us to our wedding guests. We still don't know who will officiate our service. Decisions for all those types of details will start when Mrs. Maxwell and I meet with the wedding planner.

It's going to be busy between now and the ceremony, that much is certain. I'm thankful that my schedule at Anchorage Grace Church is so flexible. In some strange and inexplicable way, I feel even busier now than I did when I was waiting tables six mornings a week.

My worries have eased when I open the doors to Pioneer Peaks. I sign in and make my way down the familiar halls. Soon, I see my mother's favorite caretaker, a friend of mine I've known since high school. For several gut-wrenchingly awful months in the past, Gus helped me wade through the terrible decision to move Mom in here or continue trying to watch over her myself, and he's been taking amazingly good care of her ever since. In high school, Gus was both popular and friendly, the type of student who'd help anybody without ever trying to draw attention to himself, and this job seems to have been tailor-made just for him. Today Gus is wearing Donald Duck scrubs and is walking toward me with a huge grin.

"Saw your smiling face in the newspaper," he declares, and I'm surprised that so many people still read the Daily News. "You're practically Alaska royalty now. You'll have to tell me how you ended up catching the eye of Anchorage's most eligible bachelor."

I let out a chuckle. "Well, if you were to believe the lies at the diner, Mrs. Maxwell paid the hostess to seat him at my table. Which is ironic since I'm convinced she hates me. Anyway, how's Mom doing?"

"Pretty good," Gus assures me with a smile. "I showed her the article, but I don't think she realized it was you."

"That's okay."

"We have some extra copies if you want to take them home."

I feel strange talking about my engagement, and I pretend it's not because of the way Gus so awkwardly asked me out shortly after Mom moved in. I'd only recently started dating James, otherwise I probably would have been thrilled at the idea. Thankfully, Gus is kind enough that he's never made me feel embarrassed for turning him down. In fact, we've just become better friends, and he's always the one I call when I'm worried about Mom or wrestling with guilt over not taking care of her myself. Still, I imagine this conversation about my engagement would feel more balanced if Gus had someone special in his life too. I've even thought about introducing him to my roommate Becca.

I decide to change the subject. "So Mom's having a good day?"

"Sharp as a whistle," Gus answers. "Hey, I'm headed to the staff room. Want me to grab you a coffee? What do you take, like eight sugars?"

"No thanks. You probably wouldn't make it sweet enough." I chuckle, thankful Mom's having a good day. I'm not sure I have the emotional energy to handle any big meltdowns. Does that make me a terrible person, I wonder. I think about the day a couple months ago when I came in to visit and she thought I was there to rob her. When I tried to calm her down, she screamed and clawed and left me with a bruised forearm and a broken heart.

"Well, go ahead and let yourself in," Gus says. "I checked on her a little bit ago, and she was in there watching TV. She mentioned something about a shower, and I told her we'd get her cleaned up this evening right after dinner like usual."

I'm glad to see Gus on shift. After everything I've been through, I could use a friendly and familiar face. Every time I end my day by jotting down bullet points in my gratitude journal, Gus is at the top of the list. He's not just my mother's caretaker, he's my confidante whenever I need to confess how miserable of a daughter I feel like I am. I could talk about my guilt with James or Becca, but as kind as they are and willing to listen, they don't fully understand. Back when Gus and I were in high school, he was taking care of his older brother, who suffered a serious brain injury in a snow machine accident. Over the course of his life, he's developed the patience and empathy that come from being a caretaker for someone you love. He's seen me at my worst, he doesn't make me feel awkward if talking about Mom's care makes me cry, and he knows how much it means to me to get honest assessments on her condition. If I need someone who won't sugarcoat the truth, I can trust Gus to give me direct answers. In fact, if I told Gus that I was taking Mom home to care for her there, he'd probably stage some kind of intervention in order to keep me from assuming a role that would mean disaster for my own well-being and physical and mental health. Becca's the friend I turn to when I need fun and diversion. James makes me feel safe and secure and loved. It's Gus who will tell me how things really are, even if it's the last thing I'm prepared or willing to hear.

Jeopardy's on in the background as I step into Mom's room. Mrs. Maxwell arranged for the florist who decorates her condo to deliver a new arrangement to the nursing home every week. Today's bouquet is new even though the flowers that were here yesterday hadn't even started to wilt. The smell of roses and lilies welcomes me into Mom's room, a pleasant heady scent that valiantly attempts to cover over the harsh antiseptic.

"Hi, Mom." I step toward her, and for a second, maybe two, I'm between breaths, hoping she's herself, afraid she's not, uncertain which version of this woman to expect.

"Hello?" Her voice sounds weak, but her eyes smile.

I take her hands in mind. "It's me, Daphne." I kneel by her chair. "How are you, Mom?"

"Well," she begins and looks around the room as if the answer is written out for her on one of the walls. "That nice young man was just here and he said something about a bath."

"That was Gus," I tell her. "He talked to you about taking a shower tonight."

"What's that, honey?" she asks, leaning closer.

I repeat myself, but she still doesn't hear or doesn't understand. I hate having to enunciate each word or repeat myself three or four times. I want to talk with her like we used to. I want to feel the way she used to brush my hair.

I want to hear the way she used to sing. I want my mother back.

"After dinner," I try again, speaking slowly as if to a small child, "my friend Gus is going to help you take a shower."

Mom frowns but her eyes remain placid. "Gus?"

I'm thrilled that she at least caught the name, which shows her brain is following a small bit of our conversation. "Yes, Gus," I repeat with a smile. "My friend from high school. He works here and helps take care of you."

"Is he the plumber?"

"No, Mom, he's a caretaker. He'll come in later and help you get clean."

"Who's clean?"

"Never mind." I sigh. Even if I got her to understand that Gus will help her shower tonight, she'll forget this conversation by dinnertime, and again I'm overcome with that suffocating guilt. Maybe I should come back tonight and wash her myself. Then I recall how I used to have to fight her to bathe before she moved in here. One day she got scared in the middle of a shower and screamed for help, shrieking that I was trying to drown her. That was the night I called Gus crying and asked him if the home he worked at had any open beds.

Mom stares at the TV then asks, "Did you get his number?"

"Whose number?"

"The plumber," she answers. "The one in here talking about ... that. In there." She gestures toward the bathroom.

"The shower? Yeah, Gus will help you shower tonight after dinner."

"I think he's a plumber, isn't he?"

I glance at the television, where today's guest host is reading an answer from the Impressionist painters category. It's too bad Mom can't follow along anymore. Ten years ago, even five, she would have gotten every single question right.

"Did he call you today, sweetie? You never told me."

"Did who call?" I ask. "Gus?"

"No, Frank. Did he call you? About his house. The small part."

"The cabin, Mom? Is that what you're saying? Are you asking about Dad's old cabin?"

"The cabin?" She speaks the word as if she's tasting it on her tongue, then she slowly shakes her head. "I don't like her going there. It's so far away."

"Don't worry, I'm not going to Dad's cabin."

"He's not healthy," Mom mumbles, and I wonder if perhaps her memory issues are a sign of God's mercy to her. "Not healthy," Mom repeats, shaking her head.

I want to talk about just about anything else. I scan the room until my eyes land on Mom's dresser. "I like those pretty flowers, Mom. Did they come today?" I repeat myself more than once, and even then I'm not sure she follows me.

"This bouquet is from James and his mom. You remember my fiancé, James?"

"Who now?"

"James. He comes sometimes with me to see you. His mom makes sure they send you these pretty flowers to keep your room nice."

"Oh." She stares vacantly at the TV, and my heart drops when I realize Mom has lost the flow of our conversation entirely.

"It's such a little house," she tells me, muttering so I can hardly make out the words. "And it's too far away when she goes there."

It's easier for Mom to talk about the past, since her long-term memories have remained more intact than anything recent. But I don't want to talk about my dad, and I don't want to think about his cabin. I want to sit with her and go through *Modern Bride* together. I want to tell her about my lunch with Mrs. Maxwell's friends, to hear her tell me that I don't need plastic surgery or laser freckle removal to be a beautiful bride.

I want to plan my wedding with this woman who raised me, not with some celebrity planner. I want her to tell me how happy she is that I found my soulmate.

I want my mom back.

I make one last attempt to shift the conversation away from my dad, and I reach over for the flower vase. "Don't you like these purple flowers, Mom? See how pretty they look?"

I hold the vase up to my nose and take an exaggerated sniff, then I extend them toward her.

"These are for me?" she asks.

"Yeah, they're for you. Do you want to smell them?"

I can tell from her face she doesn't understand.

"Smell them," I prompt, holding them up to her nose.

"Are they cooked?"

I let out a sigh and move the bouquet back to the dresser before my confused mother thinks I'm offering her a snack.

"Now where did that plumber go?" she asks, looking toward the bathroom. "He was supposed to come by and help with the water."

# CHAPTER 9

"HOW'S YOUR MOM DOING today?" James asks when he picks me up from Pioneer Peaks.

I sigh as I plop into the passenger seat beside him. "She's calm enough, so that's nice."

"Great."

James tells me about his day at the church, and I listen contentedly while he ruminates about his sermon outline for Sunday and the plans for this summer's VBS and the new youth group curriculum they'll be trying in the fall. As we drive back toward James' little parsonage in Anchorage's South Side, I'm not thinking about my parents or his parents or our wedding or whether or not I might ever find myself fitting into his church and social sphere. I relish these quiet times together and wish we didn't have that silly dinner planned with his family so we could spend a quiet evening in with just the two of us.

"Oh." Thinking about tonight reminds me of the message I was supposed to pass on. "Your mom told me she wants us there a little early. Says there's something we should talk about before dinner?" I pause, hoping James will give me a clue as to what to expect tonight at the Maxwells.

"Hmm." His response is far from elucidating. I stare out the window as we pass the golf course, the picture-perfect Hillside neighborhoods, leaving the louder and more crowded parts of Anchorage farther and farther behind us. As traffic and congestion taper off, I'm still worrying about tonight. What does Mrs. Maxwell want? Has she finally decided that I'm not good enough for her son? Was today's luncheon just the final confirmation that I'll never fit into her family life and social circle?

I try to remember exactly what words she used when she mentioned this evening. Was it just that she wanted to talk to me? Talk to us? Did she say it was something negative, or did I just assume? What if it's the exact opposite? What if she wants to meet with me and James to tell us that they're giving us the downtown condo and moving full-time to their Eagle River home? Or maybe it has to do with a wedding present. Maybe she wants to give me something so elaborate she's afraid I'll be overwhelmed, and she needs James there to convince me to accept it. My mind races as I think through the possibilities. A honeymoon in Europe? Her daughter's entire wardrobe? An appointment with Dr. van Hopper? This last image is so absurd I need to clench my jaw to keep from laughing. From the driver's seat, James glances over at me questioningly, and I cough as if I simply needed to clear my throat.

James is silent, and now I'm convinced that there's something about tonight's visit he doesn't want to tell me. "Do you have any idea what the meeting's for?" I finally press.

James sighs. "It's probably about that silly prenup. She's been working the lawyer overtime, I'm sure. I'm sorry, sweetie. I know it's not very romantic, but it's important to my family."

"Oh."

"It's not anything about you specifically," he hastens to assure me. "But I told you about my cousin's divorce, right? It was a disaster, her entire life savings cut in half, just like that. It's not a big deal, really. We had one drawn up for me and Manderley too."

I glance at him, trying not to show my surprise and unease at the mention of his ex-fiancée. I've never met her. I'm not even sure she lives in Alaska anymore. Every time I experience a serious lapse in judgment and stalk her on Instagram, she's on some kind of mission trip or charity cruise or posting from some bougie fundraiser or high-end conference in the Lower 48. I'm not entirely sure what she does, if she would call herself an influencer or fundraiser or lobbyist. I guess when you come from a family like hers, you can simply bounce from charity to charity and cause to cause without needing to label yourself. All I know is that in every single photo she looks beautiful, elegant, and poised, and based on the work she's involved in and the posts she makes, she seems to genuinely care about the hungry, the downtrodden, the world.

That's one of the problems. I want to hate her, but she's so frustratingly perfect.

James reaches over and gives my hand a squeeze. "You know what Manderley and I had is all in the past, don't you? It's just that you get weird any time someone mentions her name." I want to tell James that he's wrong, that there's no way I'm insecure enough to think twice about a girlfriend he broke up with years before I ever met him. But he knows me too well.

"What's going through that brain of yours?" he asks.

I sigh, knowing that I have to tell him the truth. "I usually don't worry about it. Not too much," I add. "But then days like this, with your mom and all her luncheon friends, and ... I don't know. I just sometimes wonder how you ended up with someone like me when the whole world would have expected you to end up with someone like her."

James holds my hand even tighter in his. "Daphne," he says, his voice full of earnest emotion, "Manderley and I grew up together. I was closer to her than to my own siblings. We were best friends until we started dating in ninth grade. That's so young. We didn't know anything then about the world and goals and what we wanted out of life and ... well ..." His voice trails off, and I hold my breath. This is the longest conversation we've ever had about the senator's Instagram-perfect daughter, and I don't want to say or do anything that might risk snapping him out of this moment of honesty.

I wish I was more mature, someone who could have a conversation like this without feeling jealous or insecure. But I can't stop myself from picking at the nagging doubt that's creeping in, not necessarily through my conscious mind. It's more like a hidden poison seeping through my capillaries and viscera, a tingling in my fingers, a gnawing in my gut. I can't put a name to it, not at this exact moment.

Or maybe it's just that I don't want to.

I need to yank myself out of this miserable funk. Manderley Danvers isn't a threat. I'm the one marrying James.

I'm the one he chose. I'm the one wearing his engagement ring on my finger, never mind the fact that a few years ago this same family heirloom was worn by someone else, someone prettier and richer and more socially acceptable than me.

"That was years ago, you know," James resumes, and I try to pretend that he and I are two secure adults talking about the past without any baggage or jealousy whatsoever. It's like I might have told him, *When I was in high school I took a biology class.* That's all there is to this. Of course I myself had crushes and even a boyfriend before James and I met, and I don't feel like I'm tiptoeing around broken glass when I mention any of them. James knows that Gus from the nursing home and I were friends at Bartlett High and went to our junior and senior proms together as part of the same large group. I've told James about my only real boyfriend who dumped me the moment I fell apart after Mom's diagnosis. When these discussions come up, they come up naturally and without any hint of embarrassment or concern.

I want to have the same type of conversation with James now about Manderley. I know they were high-school sweethearts. I know they were engaged for nearly a whole year before they broke up and that enough time has passed since then that it should allow us to discuss this part of James' past with indifference. Except that hungry, nameless speck in the pit of my stomach wants to grow, wants to raise itself to my conscious attention, wants to be seen and heard and coddled and recognized.

I sit very still, like I've just been told I can't pick at a scab, and the more I think about it the more the desire grows like an itch that threatens to steal away every semblance of peace and contentedness until you feel like you're losing your mind.

James squeezes my hand again. "You are the perfect woman for me," he assures me, "and I couldn't be prouder to have you as my bride."

A warmth rushes over me, spreading through my entire core and out to my limbs. It's enough to silence the monster of doubt, this malignant threat inside me that remains unnamed and unrecognized.

For now.

We're at the base of the Hillside when James asks, "Did that help? I don't want any secrets between us. I don't want you to worry about these things and not tell me. Is there anything else you want to know? Anything I can say or do to put your mind at rest?"

A good girlfriend, a secure girlfriend, would tell him that everything is fine, that I'm so glad we're together and I'll never give his ex another thought in the world. But James knows me too well.

"Well?" he presses.

We're just a couple minutes away from James' home by now, and I wonder if it's worth risking the question, wonder if I'm about to ruin our entire night. "I guess you never told me exactly what happened," I say. "Why you broke up."

"Oh." For just a second, there's something in my fiancé's voice. What is it? Sadness?

Regret?

Then he seems to snap himself out of whatever took hold of him and continues. "Manderley and I had different goals in life. She was into expensive dinners and high society, and I was already toying with the idea of leaving the oil business and pursuing ministry. I don't think it fit her idea of the power couple she wanted us to become."

"Did she actually say that?"

"No," James answers as we pull into the church driveway. "It was just a sense I had. One reason I never mentioned it to her is because I didn't think she'd adjust to the idea of being a pastor's wife."

*But you never asked her?* The question pops unchecked into my mind, but I clench my throat so nothing comes out.

He sighs as he rolls toward the small log cabin behind the church. "We were already starting to question things, then there was a big kerfuffle with a new bill that would have opened up more drilling. Dad's business had first rights to the area, and I guess the family expected because of our relationship that Senator Danvers would be the one to push the bill through. Instead he killed it. After that, Manderley started acting strange around me, all worried and timid like I should be mad at her."

There's something in James' words that bothers me, but I don't have time to analyze them before my phone buzzes with an incoming text.

It's my roommate Becca.

*Girl, call me ASAP. You'll never guess who I just met.*

# CHAPTER 10

JAMES PARKS IN FRONT of the parsonage, and I tell him to head on in while I call Becca back.

"Girl." Becca punctuates the word as if it were a sentence on its own, then without further greeting dives into an exposition of the customer she just served at the diner. "So I'm on the afternoon shift, and right around 4:00 or 4:30 this couple came in and sat down, nothing weird or unusual at all, right? I mean, I guess it's a little early for someone our age to be having dinner, but whatever, maybe they're tourists or something, know what I mean?

"Okay, so then I take their order and all that stuff, and they're totally normal, exactly what you'd expect, not rude, not chatty, just a couple eating an early dinner on a weeknight, except she's like super gorgeous and he's kind of whatever, but that sometimes happens, you know. Well, when I come back with their drinks, she's in the bathroom or something and he's got a paper in front of him, like the Daily News, and I'm like, *That's a little weird*. I mean, usually it's only the old regulars who come in and actually sit with a print newspaper, right?

"And I look, and he's on the page with your engagement photo, and I didn't think anything of it, and I'm just like, *Oh, look, that's my roommate right there. I'm going to be her maid of honor*, and his eyes light up, and he gets all excited like we're all of a sudden best friends, and he says something like, *Okay, so then you can tell me because I totally thought she looked familiar. Did she grow up near Eureka*, and I tell him I don't remember exactly where but you used to spend your summers camping and hiking and junk like that with your dad."

As my brain catches up with Becca's words, my stomach drops, and my hands feel clammy. I stare out over the dashboard and watch as James takes the dog out for a quick squat on the grass, and I can't find a single word to say.

I'm sure Becca has no idea what's going on in my mind as she continues as quickly as before.

"So then the girl comes back, they give me their order, the rest of dinner is totally normal, except they pay with cash and again, who under the age of sixty-five does that, right? But as they're going out I hear these whispers from a table of ladies, and they're talking about her, and I'm like, *No, it can't be.* But then I look her up on Instagram, and sure enough, you'll never guess who it was at my table."

*If only that were true*, I think to myself. I'm so exhausted it's hard to conjure up any emotional reaction whatsoever.

"It was Manderley Danvers." Becca's laugh is grating. "And she and that new guy of hers were both totally fishing for information on you." She lowers her voice. "And I mean, who can blame her? To go from James Maxwell to some skinny nerd like that? Oof. I just love the thought of her seeing your engagement photo and being so stinking jealous she came all the way to where you used to work. I bet she was hoping to dig up dirt on you, don't you think? When she left it was like I needed an extra rag just to wipe off all that envy she left behind."

Becca pauses, and my mind is still racing to catch up. I literally have nothing to say.

"Here." Becca fills in the silence. "I snuck a photo of them as soon as I realized who they were. You've got to see this guy she's with."

My body is reacting on auto-pilot when my cell vibrates and I look at the image she just texted.

"See what I mean?" Becca asks. "Talk about how the mighty have fallen, right?"

But I don't answer, because I know this guy. It's the so-called random stranger from the coffee shop, the one who said he knew my dad.

"Daphne?" Becca is saying. "You alright? Trust me, you have absolutely nothing to be worried about. I've seen her up close, and that girl has nothing on you."

I let my brain come up with some preprogrammed response just to get Becca to stop talking. I need a minute. I need time alone to figure out what all this means. I glance at the image on my phone once more, thinking I might be wrong.

But I'm not. The man in the photo is wearing the same Fairbanks hoodie, has the same tall, lanky frame. It's Clark, the guy from Kaladi Brothers.

But what does it mean?

Is Manderley spying on me? But why? I think about my conversation with Clark in the coffee line, and then it hits me.

Clark knows who my father is. Which means that now Manderley does too.

# CHAPTER 11

My legs are heavy when I let myself out of James' car and head up toward his front porch. I need time to let everything Becca told me sink in, time to figure out what it means, if anything.

The problem is I have no time. In a few seconds, I'll be inside the parsonage with James, and I'll either have to pretend nothing's wrong or tell him everything and risk sounding insane. Couldn't the entire thing be one big mix-up?

I pull up the photo Becca sent to my cell. I can see Clark in his Fairbanks hoodie. I know it's the same guy. Manderley's back is to us, and now that I look at the picture again, I couldn't even tell if it's her. She has shiny black hair, flawless really, but besides that, she could be anyone.

Okay, so maybe this isn't even Manderley. Maybe Becca's wrong.

But still, it can't be a coincidence that just a few hours after we meet at the coffee shop this same strange guy comes up, seated at my roommate's table, and asking questions about me, right?

So what are the possible explanations? Maybe Manderley's checking up on me, but what do she and Clark have to do with each other? Or maybe the woman from the diner isn't Manderley at all, but that still doesn't provide any clues why Clark's fishing for information about me and my dad.

A coincidence? Could the entire thing be just some random string of events? Anchorage isn't that big of a town, and of course Becca loves to gossip, so as soon as she saw him looking at the newspaper she would have wanted to tell him about me.

Could it all be as simple as that? Clark knows my family. When Becca said she was my roommate, wouldn't it make sense for him to ask another question or two, even just to be polite?

Something still isn't sitting right with me, but I can't stand around worrying all night. In just over an hour we've got to get back on the road and make our way to James' parents for dinner. Whatever's going on with these strangers at the diner, I'll have to mull over it while I go about the rest of the night.

I just hope James is preoccupied and doesn't notice me sinking into this quagmire of questions and possibilities and doubts. If I told him I thought his ex-girlfriend was sitting at my old diner and picking my roommate's brain for my personal information, I'd sound crazy.

Paranoid.

I'd sound like my father.

When I open the front door of James' small parsonage, his springer spaniel rushes toward me. Jasper jumps up, trying to kiss my face even though he's too wiggly to actually achieve his goal, and I'm thankful for a cheerful distraction. If I'm still unsettled about my conversation with Becca, I'll bring it up to James later, maybe on the way to his parents' tonight, maybe tomorrow evening when we don't have anything planned, at least not as far as I can remember.

For right now, I need time to think, and I need this welcome diversion while Jasper wriggles to press as much of his body up against me as possible.

"The way he's acting, you'd think he hasn't seen you in years. Isn't that right, buddy?" James adds as he leans down toward his dog. Jasper's docked tail wags animatedly.

I make my voice sound as casual as possible when I ask, "Is there anything I can do at the church since I'm here?"

James' back is to me as he fills Jasper's dinner bowl to the accompaniment of happy, exultant barks, and I feel myself relaxing piece by piece. I do my best to banish all thoughts of Manderley to the overflowing junk drawer in my mind.

While Jasper eats greedily, James considers my question. "You know, since we've got a little time, I'd love if you could look over my board recommendation letter, make sure it all makes sense and doesn't have any spelling mistakes."

When I first met James, I assumed he spent his days reading the Bible and visiting members of his congregation, offering them prayer and encouragement. Once I started working with him at the office, I was surprised to realize how much energy he spends just on admin, from overseeing the church's various ministries to keeping board members happy to making sure the bills get paid on time. At least my job at Anchorage Grace isn't only ceremonial — a pity position created for the poor girl with a sick mom, and I'm glad for whatever chance I get to lighten his load.

I picture the two of us after we're married, when this log cabin is my home. James will step inside after a long day at the office and feed Jasper, and I'll be seated at the table, working on something important. I'll look up and give him a smile, and we'll both feel so happy to see each other, even though we've never been more than about a hundred feet apart all day long.

"Sure." I stand up, happy for something useful to do. "Is it on the church computer?"

"Oh, I've got it here," James says. "I emailed myself a copy." He opens up his laptop and logs in. "Here you go." He turns his back to me and starts loading some cups and plates into the dishwasher.

Truth be told, I was hoping for a few quiet moments alone at the church, but as I situate myself at the kitchen counter, I'm thankful that James is busy. Even a short distraction before he and I dive into any type of deep conversation will help ensure the junk drawer in my mind stays closed.

The letter I'm reading is James' proposal to increase the church's missionary budget at the start of the new fiscal year. I'm proud that my future husband has such a generous soul and heart for missions. The points he spells out, including Bible verses for each argument, make me wonder why the church didn't adopt a policy like this years earlier. Even though I'm not the best editor in the world, James has assured me multiple times that the feedback I give him is indispensable, and while I reread his letter I picture us twenty years from now, still in this small parsonage, the house filled with photographs of our children and trinkets collected from the life we've made together.

*You know*, James would say, *that feedback you gave me on my Mother's Day sermon was so spot on. I lost count of how many women, and even some men too, came up to me afterward and told me how much it meant to them.*

*Yes*, I imagine myself answering, *it's so important for pastors to have an understanding of what people with complicated pasts go through on a day like this. It's not as simple of a holiday as Hallmark makes it sound.*

I picture James leaning over, kissing the top of my head, telling me what a great team we make, how he couldn't possibly do his ministry without me. And I'll smile across our cozy little breakfast nook, sipping the coffee he's poured for me (although he never makes it quite sweet enough), and remind him that he was already a beloved and respected pastor before we were ever married. And he'd smile back at me and sigh and say something like, *How did I ever manage on my own?*

My romantic musings are interrupted when a popup appears in the bottom corner of his laptop. When I read the accompanying name, my very first, somewhat sacrilegious reaction is, *Come on, Jesus. You've got to be kidding me.*

My heart is racing, and I must have made some type of gasp or noise, because James is by my side in an instant, staring over my shoulder. The notification disappears, but not before both James and I have a chance to read it.

*Direct message from Manderley Danvers: James, we have to speak.*

Even though my body's responding as if I were being charged by a brown bear, I clench my fists, take a deep breath, and remind myself there are plenty of innocuous reasons why James' ex-girlfriend might be trying to get in touch. Maybe she's heard about our engagement and wants to congratulate him. After all, they've been family friends for basically their entire lives. It might even be something that proves her trip to the diner was nothing but coincidence. *Hi James, long time! Most random thing in the world happened today ... I was out to lunch with a friend and our waitress is your fiancée's roommate! Small world, right? Anyway, congrats to you both.*

Then again, it might not have to do with me at all. Maybe Manderley has news about someone they both knew from school, or has a friend who wants to know more about his church.

*James, we have to speak.* Not exactly the type of language you'd use to casually get in touch with a friend from the past.

James doesn't move, and for a moment I'm afraid he'll be angry with me, if he thinks I was prying in his inbox, trying to spy on him. If he thinks I don't trust him.

"It just popped up," I explain lamely.

James remains silent. I can feel the tension in his entire body as he leans over my shoulder. He takes the mouse from me, right clicks, and hits block user.

"There." He straightens up.

"What if it's something important?" I ask.

"I seriously doubt that." James stares at me, and the following silence makes me feel guilty, like I'm a naughty child caught snooping where I don't belong.

Jasper whines at the door, begging to be let out, and I jump on the opportunity to get away from this laptop as if it were a fatal poison with the power to kill.

"Want me to take him out for a short you-know-what?" I ask. Even without me speaking the word directly, Jasper's eyes light up and he runs to the leash hanging in the entryway, letting out one shrill, excited yelp.

James slips on his shoes. "Let's both go," he says, while Jasper hops exultantly at his heels. "I could use some fresh air."

# CHAPTER 12

THE SUMMER SUN SHINES bright on the Anchorage hillside, working hard to melt away my fears and anxieties one at a time. While James and I stroll down the trail behind the parsonage, Jasper bounds about eagerly, trying to eat every blade of grass and early summer crocus we pass. The sound of my fiancé's laughter as he watches his dog wagging his stump is a healing distraction that reminds me no matter what happens, James and I will be okay.

I wish we had the entire evening for ourselves, nowhere to go, nobody to see. I imagine every single summer of my life just like this, walking the dog (or one day in the future pushing a baby stroller), with James by my side, the gentle Anchorage breeze keeping us cool while the sun beats down and warms our souls.

James is quiet, hopefully as content with the silence as I am. I try not to read more into it, try not to worry that he'll think it's suspicious I'm not talking. I know he doesn't like it when I keep my thoughts to myself, but sometimes like tonight I need time alone with my musings before I can fully recognize them myself, let alone try to explain them to someone else.

In a way, it should be so simple to tell my future husband, this man I love, what's on my mind. *What are you thinking about?* I imagine him asking me.

*Oh, just about that message you got tonight from Manderley. What do you think she wanted?*

And he'd tell me, and no matter what he responded, I'd hear his voice and know with certainty that all my fears and all my doubts and all my insecurities were completely baseless. I wouldn't even need to hear the words themselves, just the way he said them, and in his expression I'd make out the one truth I long to cling to more than anything: *Daphne, you are the love of my life, and nothing will ever come between us. Not now and not ever. When did you start worrying about all this?*

And I'd tell him about how Becca thought she saw Manderley at the diner, and we'd laugh, reminding ourselves that even though Anchorage is the largest city in the state, everything in Alaska can feel like a small town from time to time, so that even if it was his ex seated at my roommate's table, it was nothing more than a strange coincidence.

In my head, the conversation sounds so simple. James is a reasonable man, and his emotional maturity is one of the traits I adore most about him.

I could mention it all.

But I don't.

In a valiant attempt to banish Manderley Danvers completely from my thoughts, I focus my attention on Jasper, who's tugging on the leash and sniffing at a pile of leaves on the side of the trail. He'd grown a bit chubby last winter, but now that we're taking him on regular walks again, his body is sleek and agile, and his shiny coat glistens healthily. I never really considered myself a dog person, not until Jasper. He was a bit shy around me when we first met, but I won him over that very first day with the puppy ice cream cups that James keeps stocked for special occasions. Now if James and I arrive at the parsonage together I'm often the first person to be greeted by that happy, wagging stump of a tail or kissed on the face by a jumping, wiggling bundle of chaos. More than a small portion of his recent weight was my fault, the way I can't resist it when he begs me for treats.

I've done the math. Jasper was a puppy when James and Manderley were engaged. Was he mistrustful of her too at first? Or did she win him over immediately? Does he still miss her sometimes, I wonder.

James looks at me quizzically, and I'm not sure if he said something or asked something and is waiting for a response. I try to rewind my brain, but nothing comes up.

"What'd you say?" I ask.

"I wanted to know what you're thinking about."

"Oh." I let out a laugh that I hope sounds genuine. "I was actually just thinking about Jasper as a pup." I'm thankful that I don't have to come up with a lie. "He must have been adorable." Maybe I can ask James to show me pictures. Maybe I'll see Manderley in the background, get a better feel for how the two of them were together. Manderley and the dog, that is.

James doesn't respond, and again I try not to let his silence unsettle me. Aren't a lot of our evening walks quiet like this? Both of us enjoying nature and each other's company without feeling pressure to keep up a constant stream of conversation.

We've reached the fork in the trail, turn around in unspoken agreement, and I try to find something, anything to think about that isn't Manderley Danvers. Wedding dresses, our as-of-yet undecided honeymoon destination, the church programs I need to print up before Sunday ... I'm certain a squirrel could find something to focus on better than I can at this exact moment.

My phone beeps in my pocket. James' cell alerts at the same time, and for a moment I'm certain that Manderley Danvers has got my number somehow and is sending both of us an angry, threatening text. How dare I steal her man, how dare James walk away from the best thing that's ever happened to him, I'll never be able to fit in with the Maxwell way of life, I should have never agreed to date him, let alone marry him.

But it's not Manderley. It's Mrs. Maxwell.

*James and Daphne, Logan has arrived. Please meet us here at your earliest convenience as per our previous discussion.*

James has stopped walking, and Jasper whimpers expectantly, anxious to get home where he's no doubt planning on a delicious ice cream cup.

I check the clock on my cell. Are we late? I didn't think we were expected downtown until 7:30. Had Mrs. Maxwell changed the time? Had she given me a message to pass onto James and I completely spaced out? My pulse quickens as I try to recall.

I remember talking to Mrs. Maxwell about tonight, but I have no clue where we discussed it or what she said or anything other than the fact that it happened. My hands are clammy as I cling to Jasper's leash. What age was Mom when stuff like this started happening to her? How old was she when she shifted from a sometimes absent-minded mother to an officially diagnosed early-onset Alzheimer's patient? Is this exactly how it started with her? Meetings here and there she simply forgot about completely? Names she was supposed to remember but couldn't?

I read Mrs. Maxwell's text again, desperate for clues.

"Who's Logan?" I finally ask James.

A look of sadness crosses his face. Sadness ... or maybe concern? The parsonage has come back into view, and Jasper jumps in circles with excitement at the sight of home.

*Logan. Who in the world is Logan?* Maybe James has told me on a dozen different occasions, and I've forgotten each and every time. For a moment, I think about confessing everything, about how scared I am that I might be losing my mind. Might be losing myself. But we've had this conversation before. James figures that if I'm so concerned, I should ask the doctor for the screening test that will tell me if Mom's gene has been passed down to me or not. I either have it or I don't. The reason I refuse is the test won't just tell me that I might have a predisposition to Alzheimer's. It's a test that, if I'm shown to have the wrong gene, would guarantee I'll go through the same stages of mental decline and confusion and paranoia that Mom has, until eventually I'll be a completely different person, hardly recognizable to myself, let alone anyone else.

If I take the test and the doctor tells me I'm doomed, there's no surgery to eliminate the plaques that may have already started to form in my brain, empty space instead of the biological stuff that makes me who I am.

Who would want to know if they're destined for that type of cursed fate?

Jasper's tugging so frantically he's about to knock me over. James sighs and unclasps the leash. Jasper rushes to the parsonage, yipping triumphantly.

James has stopped walking and is looking down at me. I can't tell what's in his expression. I feel like I should apologize, although I can't guess what for.

After a moment, James lets out another sigh and continues toward the front porch, where Jasper is jumping in circles while he waits for us to catch up.

"Logan's one of the family lawyers. It must be about that stupid prenup." There's annoyance in his voice, but I don't know if it's directed at me or the dog or his mother or the attorney or something else entirely.

"Oh." I'm not exactly sure what I feel at the moment. Relief that perhaps I didn't forget something massively important? Hesitation about sitting down with the Maxwells and hammering out something as tedious and intimidating as a premarital contract? Of course I'll sign what they give me, but that doesn't explain why James looks so upset.

He sighs and picks up his pace. "Come on," he tells me, "let's put Jasper inside and get going. You know how much my mom hates to be kept waiting."

# CHAPTER 13

As James and I drive back to his parents' condo downtown, I try not to read too much into the silence. James is often quiet like this at the end of a long day. While the summer sunlight streams in through the passenger window, I'm no longer thinking about Manderley Danvers or James or the Maxwells. I'm a little girl who's just come home after spending the summer with my dad, and Mom has just finished singing her favorite hymn as she works the knots out of my unruly hair.

"You know, Daphne," Mom says, her voice so clear and bright in the years before her sickness took hold, "I love the way your freckles jump out after you've been outside in the sun. Have I ever told you how pretty they make you look?"

I'm old enough to know I shouldn't act vain. I'm also old enough to know that mothers have to say this kind of thing to their daughters, but still the compliment warms my tummy like a cup of hot chocolate.

Mom goes back to singing. I love the sound of her voice.

"Mama?" I ask, interrupting. "What's so scary about stairs?"

"Stairs?" she repeats.

"Yeah, you know, in the song you were singing. *Through many dangers, toils, and stairs.* Is that like the stairway to heaven? Or ..." I lower my voice. "Is it talking about stairs to the other place?"

Mom lets out a chuckle. "It's not about stairs, sweetie. It's about *snares.* Out of everybody your age, you should know more about snares than just about anyone."

I think about the rabbit traps I help my dad with all summer long. I don't get what they might have to do with some old song about heaven, but thinking about the traps my father sets out reminds me of something entirely different.

"You wanna hear something, Mama?"

"What's that, sweetie?"

I love the feel of Mom's soft fingers on my hair. Even if it takes us two hours to get these tangles out, she hardly ever pulls, and if she tugs too hard on accident she always says she's sorry and gives me lots of hugs and kisses before she starts again. I don't tell her that the pulling doesn't even hurt. Actually, I like when she fusses over me, like I'm still tiny and might cry if she's not extra careful.

"Did I tell you about the traps I helped Daddy make?"

"For the bunnies?" she asks. "Yeah, you told me."

I don't bother correcting her language. Bunnies are what city people have in their homes as pets. They're cute and cuddly and can't survive on their own. Rabbits are what Dad traps, what keeps him alive all winter. They're nothing like the fluffy bunnies in pet stores. The rabbits Dad catches are big, big enough to feed a man in the middle of winter. Once he said he trapped one that was as huge as a sled dog. He showed me the fur from it, and it was so big I could have wrapped it around myself and worn it like a caveman dress.

"No, Mama," I explain. "I'm not talking about the rabbit snares. Daddy and me made a trap for Bigfoot."

"Bigfoot, huh?"

I glance at her face in the mirror, but I can't tell what she's thinking.

"Yeah, except Daddy has another name for him, I just can't remember what it is right now. It's a native name, the one he uses. Last winter a Bigfoot came and tried to steal his bear meat, so this winter he's got to be more careful and make sure to set out bigger traps."

Mom stops brushing. "Just how big are these traps?"

I shrug and hold out my hands to show her. "I dunno, kinda like this." I stop when I see her worried expression. "It's just for fun, Mama. I'm too old to believe in Bigfoot."

Mom seems to relax a bit, so I know I've said the right thing.

"And I'm careful when I help him," I add. "Daddy doesn't put them out until it's winter anyway, so they can't hurt me even though they're so big. I don't think Daddy believes in Bigfoot either. It's just for fun. But I guess the traps could keep him safe if the bad guys ever show up for him."

Mom pauses with the comb in her hand. "What bad guys?"

"You know, Mama." I think about how patient she is brushing my hair, and I try not to roll my eyes. Daddy's right. He tells me that city people, even the ones we love like Mama, won't ever fully understand. That's why he lives out alone all year long, so people can't tell him he's silly for being careful.

"Why don't you tell me about the bad guys Daddy's worried about."

I glance at Mom. She gives me a smile, but I can tell she's concerned about something. I'm not sure how much I'm supposed to tell her. Daddy says you can't trust anybody, especially not city people, but Mama's different, right?

She leans close to me, smiling for real this time. "Are they quite scary?" she asks, and gives me a little tickle by my ribs.

I squeal. "No, they're not scary. But Daddy says that one day they're gonna tell him he can't live out there in the woods, that it's the government's land, and they're gonna tell him he has to leave and become a city person who has to shave his beard and shop at grocery stores and things."

Mom's eyes widen playfully. "Oh no," she says with an exaggerated gasp. "Not a big bad grocery store!"

We giggle, and it feels so good laughing with my mom. I want to find ways to keep this moment lasting forever.

"Did you and Daddy love each other a lot?" I ask, hoping this will bring her good memories.

"We did."

"You still love him lots?" I press.

Mom sighs. "Your father came into my life when I was young and confused about a lot of things, and he was there for me. And most important, he gave me you." She kisses the top of my head.

"And the reason you don't live with him anymore is because he's not a city person." I'm proud of myself for being able to talk about these things with Mama like a grownup. "But you still love him, right?"

"Yes, sweetie, there's a big part of me that will always love your daddy. And I'm glad you get to spend time with him each summer. It's just that ..."

I feel my body squeezing tight, like Mama's about to say something I don't want to hear and I need to shut my ears before the words come out.

"Oh, never mind." Mom is frowning at a big mass of tangles behind my ear, but I'm not worried about my hair. We could always cut it short if the knots are too bad. I want Mom to tell me more about Dad. I want to hear about how she ended up moving here to be a city person even though she still loves him and he still lives so far away. I hold my breath, hoping that maybe if I'm very still and very good, Mom will say something more. Turns out I'm right.

"I just want you to be careful," Mom says. "Your dad, he sometimes has funny ideas about things. Things that aren't entirely real."

"Like Bigfoot?" I press. "Mama, I told you, that was a joke. We were just making rabbit snares, only bigger."

Part of me wants Mom to say more, but I already know what it'll be.

"I know what's real and what isn't," I promise her. "And Daddy does too. Like one night he saw a UFO, except it wasn't aliens and things because those don't exist, but instead it was scientists doing tests in a huge balloon so they can do things to the weather like make it rain in places that need rain, or maybe make it winter for those poor kids in the Lower 48 who don't get any snow at Christmas."

Mom lets out a sigh. Somehow I thought that mentioning how Dad doesn't believe in aliens would prove my point, would make her fears go away, but I think I was wrong. Sensing I made some kind of mistake, I do my best to cheer her up. "Don't you think that'd be nice?" I prompt. "You know, for those kids at Christmas?"

She nods, but I don't think she's really listening to me. After a silent pause, she's singing again, and the words to *Amazing Grace* float around me, and my mother's beautiful voice wraps me up like a cozy blanket on a cold winter day.

A few minutes later, she's running the hottest bath I can stand. She goes out to make us both some dinner, but as I soak in the scalding water, I think that Dad's wrong about one thing. City people aren't all crazy or wicked or brainwashed. The woods are nice, and it's a fun way to spend a few weeks each summer, but then I like coming home to this hot bath, to the sound of my mom singing in the other room.

I listen to Mom's voice ringing out in my memory, and I know I'm truly home. I want that sense of calm and welcome to last forever, but it doesn't. We're downtown now, pulling in front of the Maxwells' condo.

"Come on," James says, his voice devoid of any emotion. "Let's get this meeting over with."

# CHAPTER 14

THE MAXWELLS' LAWYER SPREADS some papers out on the mahogany desk in the family's den. The sunlight from an ornate crystal window casts beautiful rainbows on the wood.

"All right," Logan begins. Her voice is both young and fresh. With her feathered hoop earrings, form-fitting pantsuit, and bright teal blouse, she's not at all who I was picturing when James said we were meeting with his parents' attorney. She clicks the bottom of her pen several times in quick succession, a tic I'm certain she doesn't even notice.

"Before we dive into the terms of the agreement, I want to give you my little pre-prenup pep talk."

I squeeze James' hand. Mrs. Maxwell stands unsmiling by the window, her entire body radiating displeasure. I imagine she's angry because her husband failed to show up, leaving her to manage this meeting alone. I also wonder if she's upset because signing this piece of paper will bring James and me one step closer to marriage. It seems as though every time I find myself feeling closer to Mrs.

Maxwell, something happens to remind me that I'm not the type of bride she would have ever envisioned or chosen for her son. I'm not up on all the political gossip or fashion trends like her friends from lunch. In fact Phillipa, the Maxwells' hired help, most definitely knows more about how to act and dress and behave at that type of social gathering than I do. I'm not elegant and pedigreed like Manderley Danvers. I'm a poor waitress with a deceased, deranged father and an ailing mother with dementia.

Logan is focusing on James and me instead of Mrs. Maxwell. I find myself dazzled by her earrings, which swing back and forth with every word she enunciates. "So," she continues brightly, "what everybody in this room wants and fully expects is for the both of you to have a beautifully happy engagement period, a beautifully happy wedding ceremony, and a beautifully happy life together. But we also want to go into this with our eyes wide open. Some couples find the idea of a prenup distasteful since it's written as if there's an expectation of separation somewhere down the line. The way I see it, you two have already given each other a verbal commitment to love one another for the rest of your lives. And on your wedding day, you'll sign a document that makes those vows legally binding.

"Now, here's where the prenup comes in, and does so in a way that I encourage you both to look at it as a romantic gesture emanating from love and trust and mutual respect. Daphne, by signing this agreement, you're telling James that you love him for who he is, not because of any financial gain you hope to get out of your union with him. You're telling him, *I love you so much that I want the world ... or at least our close family members and lawyers ... to know that my love for you is completely separate from any monetary benefits this relationship may bring me.* And basically, James is saying the same thing to you. Does that make sense?"

I glance at James and his mother to see if they're giving any cues. He nods somewhat stoically, but Mrs. Maxwell's back remains to us as she stares out the window. I can't begin to imagine what she might be thinking.

"Prenups are especially important," Logan continues, "in cases where one partner is bringing in a significant amount of wealth compared to the other."

I feel my face heat up. Mrs. Maxwell slowly turns around. "I think we all understand." Regally, she makes her way toward the desk and stands behind the lawyer.

"Good." Logan clicks her pen cap, seemingly oblivious to her employer's glare, and points to the first page of her document spread out on the ornate desk. "So, the first section I want to go over is the non-disparagement clause." Her pen taps the bullet point. "This section goes into effect as soon as it's signed. In other words, it's applicable in the case of divorce, separation, or if the wedding gets called off."

Behind her, I think I see Mrs. Maxwell smirk. Or maybe I'm just imagining it.

Logan points to the first bold line on her document and reads the first clause out loud. "Both parties agree not to make any disparaging remarks or comments, whether in public or private, about each other, their families, or their relationship. Pretty standard stuff," she adds as an aside.

That's not too hard to understand, I realize. Maybe this won't be so bad after all.

"Next," Logan continues, "we've got the gift return provision. This section remains in effect until three months following your wedding. If the wedding is canceled or if the marriage ends in annulment, legal separation, or divorce within the first three months of your union, this clause states that all wedding, engagement, and bridal shower presents, whether received individually or jointly, shall be returned if at all reasonably possible. In other words, if Daphne's great-aunt Sally gives you both a blender before the wedding and then you call off the engagement, or if she gives you a toaster at your wedding and then you annul your relationship, separate, or divorce within the first three months, it's your shared responsibility to return the appliances to her in as close to their original condition as reasonably possible. It's the same thing with any monetary gifts or cash received."

I feel myself relax slightly. If the entire document is this simple, we can have it signed and forgotten before the rest of James' family arrives for dinner.

Logan continues reading the bullet points in the document, taking time to explain some of the legal jargon and giving hypothetical examples about when and how these clauses would be enforced. Nothing seems nearly as harsh or intimidating as I initially feared, so I allow my mind to wander. Her words float over and around me like a mist. I'm tired. The sunshine outside is bright, and my hand is sweaty as I hold onto James. While Logan talks about debt and property ownership and lifestyle maintenance, I think about how I'd redo this office if we ever took over this condo.

Assuming James didn't want this room for his pastor's study, I picture what I'd have to change to turn it into an art studio. The ornate rug would be the first thing to go. It looks like it's older than my mom, and there's no reason to have something that expensive on the floor just to get paint splattered on it. Then again, maybe I'd decide to channel my inner Jackson Pollock and decorate the entire rug with paint splatter. I almost giggle to myself when I picture Mrs. Maxwell's shock if she could read my mind, if she knew what I'm thinking of doing to this stuffy, pretentious office.

The desk is beautiful, but it takes up so much space. I'd slide it out of the way, over there to the left where there's good lighting. I imagine it'd work well for a drawing table. Or maybe that's where I'd run the business side of my creative empire. I could make designs to sell on Etsy, or maybe I'd become a children's author and illustrator and use the desk for writing and the other half of the office for painting. There's an adjoining deck that overlooks the inlet, and I can picture myself stepping out for some fresh air to give my creative mind a break before returning to work.

There's something deeply masculine about the dark mahogany bookshelves, but I can't decide if that's the heaviness of the wood itself or the densely packed law and business books stuffed onto them. There's enough sunlight streaming in that the shelf would be great for some plants. One summer when I was in high school, Mom and I painted hundreds of terracotta pots and sold them at the Alaska State Fair. Maybe I could do something similar, but this time instead of selling my art I'd fill them with rare and beautiful plants to breathe life into this drab room.

"Okay, so what we just went over is basic stuff that goes into nearly every prenup, then there's space for certain clauses specific to the couple in question." Logan fixes her gaze at me. "I understand, Daphne, that your mother, Mrs. Winters, is a full-time resident in a care facility?"

I glance at James, trying to determine if he's as confused as I am. What does my mother's care have to do with any of this?

"Yes, she has early-onset dementia," I manage to answer. Is this about the genetic screening? Are the Maxwells going to make me get my DNA tested before they let their son marry someone who might be incoherent and incontinent in three more decades, before I can embarrass the family name or pass my mother's disease on to their grandchildren?

Logan nods. "Given your delicate situation, the family has decided ..."

"I'll explain," Mrs. Maxwell interrupts. She's been quiet for so long that her stately form has morphed into the background, and I'm surprised to hear her speak. My cheeks flush, as if she's caught me stealing food from her pantry. "Daphne." Mrs. Maxwell levels her gaze. "We want to make sure your mother is well taken care of. Part of our engagement gift to you and to James is that we have established a trust to ensure your mother's care for the remainder of her life. She can stay where she is, of course, but if you'd prefer, there are nicer facilities or private care options that will now be available to you. We can discuss the details later, but these funds have been made available to you for her care effective immediately."

I don't know what to say. James looks as surprised as I am.

"Wow," I finally state. "That's, well, that's really kind. And generous. Thank you so much."

Mrs. Maxwell waves her hand in the air dismissively. "You can go on with the other points," she tells Logan before turning her back to us to stare outside, and I feel like I've just been given a reprimand instead of such a huge and unexpected gift.

Logan shoots another apologetic glance my way, and I feel my body tense. The next several clauses are so convoluted and full of financial jargon my brain is growing heavier and foggier by the moment, so that simply listening to each sentence carries the mental weight of writing a college essay paper. Is this how Mom felt when her Alzheimer's first kicked in, unable to follow the flow of a conversation, embarrassed to admit it even to herself?

While Logan drones on about retirement accounts and spousal support and splitting assets, I wish I could ask Mom about her engagement period. My parents held a Christian ceremony but never registered their marriage with the state. Dad was already mistrustful of the government, even though his paranoia and illness didn't manifest themselves entirely until later. Mom hadn't turned into a full-fledged "city person" yet, so neither of my parents saw any reason to get legal permission to commit their lives to one another. As unconventional and bohemian as their relationship might have been, I can see its appeal when you compare its informality to the cold, hard legalese James and I are wading through.

"Now we've added a non-disclosure clause here," Logan goes on. "Basically, it states that whether you are engaged, married, separated, or divorced, neither of you will divulge any sensitive information about each other. So in your case, Daphne, this means you wouldn't speak publicly or on social media about any matters pertaining to the Maxwells' family business."

"We have certain proprietary arrangements," Mrs. Maxwell explains. "And we've learned that we can never be too careful with whom we trust." Mrs. Maxwell levels her gaze at me, and I feel as if I'm a little child being punished for an offense I haven't committed yet.

Logan clears her throat and adds in a somewhat quieter voice, "There's one more section in this clause that I hope is understandable without having to go into details. But it also states, Daphne, that when you are in public you will refrain from talking about, writing about, or posting on social media anything about your father."

# CHAPTER 15

THE DINNER GUESTS HAVE already started to arrive by the time we sign all the forms and leave the office. Soon the Maxwell home is even more crowded than it was at lunch. James' parents, his brother and sister-in-law, and two or three dozen friends and colleagues are all seated together, talking over each other while the staff serves up one course after another, crab cakes and London broil and Alaska prawns, with crème brûlée for dessert.

The conversation is mercifully inane, and my brain has time to wander while the various discussions float around me — politics, finance, local gossip, nothing that holds my interest or requires my input. James is seated on my left, and he seems to know I need time alone with my thoughts. On my right is some businessman or politician who completely ignores me while trying to ingratiate himself with Mr. Maxwell and the more obviously important guests.

In spite of the mental respite during the meal, I still find myself seeking solace on the balcony overlooking the inlet once everyone migrates to the living room for coffee and drinks. It's almost nine o'clock, but the summer sun still shines as bright as midday and glistens on the coast.

"Pretty evening, isn't it?" James comes up beside me and hands me a glass of sparkling cider. Without waiting for an answer, he puts his arm around me and lets out a deep sigh. "Well, nice to have that over," he declares contentedly.

"What, the dinner?" I ask.

James gives a small chuckle. "No, that stupid prenup. Thanks for not going all crazy over it." He lowers his voice. "I didn't know they were going to bring up ..." He stops himself and clears his throat. "I didn't know what it said until tonight."

I shrug. If signing a stupid piece of paper makes Mrs. Maxwell feel better about me marrying her son, so be it. And if a prenup helps silence any gossip that I'm just a gold digger out to stake my claim in the Maxwell fortune, it's all for the best. I shouldn't feel upset that they mentioned my dad. It makes sense even to me, at least on a logical level. James' family is involved in business and politics all over the state. If word got out that their youngest son was engaged to the daughter of Frank Chilkoot ...

"Are you cold?" James asks when I let out a small shiver.

I shake my head. "No." I turn to him and force a smile. Here in the summer breeze, standing next to my fiancé and overlooking the peaceful Cook Inlet, I'm reminded just how blessed I truly am. I think about all those prayers Mom offered up for me and wonder if this is a moment I'll remember for the rest of my life with James.

"You look sad." He reaches out and touches my cheek. As hard as I was trying to put on a cheerful air, he sees right through me.

I'm not sad, at least I don't think I am. But it's been such a busy day, I actually don't know how I feel. I'm glad that the parsonage where James and I will settle down is on the opposite side of Anchorage. I can't picture myself being downtown all the time, with these huge get-togethers and lack of privacy.

James leans over and kisses the top of my head. I take his hand, about to resign myself to joining the rest of the guests in the living room, when my phone rings. I don't recognize the number, but it's local.

I hold up the screen. "This might be the nursing home." I try not to jump directly into panic mode, but my heart is already speeding up.

James gives me a soft smile. "I'll be inside when you're done. Take your time."

I watch him retreat back into his parents' home and say a quick prayer for my mom before I answer. "Hello?"

There's silence for a moment, and I imagine all the worst scenarios. A policeman calling to tell me my mom had a horrible accident and is in an ambulance on her way to the hospital. An orderly calling to say Mom's wandered off the premises and is lost somewhere in midtown Anchorage. The manager of the nursing home calling to personally beg me to come calm down my mom after one of her paranoid spells.

"Is this Daphne?"

I've only heard her voice before from the few videos I've watched online, but immediately I know who it is. I'm not sure if I manage to answer her question before my voice freezes in my throat.

"Daphne, this is Manderley Danvers." Another pause. Does she sound scared?

My thumb is hovering over the red end call button when I hear, "Don't hang up. It's about your dad."

When I find my voice, it's warbly and weak. "How did you get my number?"

"I'm working with an investigative journalist," she tells me. "You met him. At Kaladi Brothers."

I think about the stranger in the Fairbanks hoodie from the coffee shop. Figures.

My body has dumped adrenaline into each vein and pore and capillary, and my mind begins to flit from one possible explanation to another. She's going to threaten me, tell me she'll let everyone know who my dad is if I don't break up with James. Or maybe she doesn't want James to herself anymore, but she's going to blackmail us both — monthly payments in exchange for her silence. Sadly, knowing what I know about the Maxwells, they likely would be willing to pay to keep my past a secret and save them all from public embarrassment.

*James Maxwell.* I can just imagine the tongues wagging. *First he abandoned the family business to become a pastor of all things. Then he meets some poor, penniless girl. Did you know who her father was? He was that crazy mountain man who died in that cabin fire.*

If I was bolder, if I was someone more confident, I would hang up on her now, either that or demand an explanation or complain about this intrusive violation. But I'm not bold. I'm not confident, and my voice — and my courage — have all but disappeared. I glance back to the patio door, wishing for James to sense my need, to come out here and take this phone from me and have this conversation in my stead.

But I'm here alone, and nobody is going to rescue me.

"Tell me why you're calling." My voice sounds stronger than I feel, but I still worry she'll know I'm bluffing.

"Listen." There's an earnestness in her voice, but I won't let myself respond to her manipulations. "Your dad had information about my father," she continues, and for a brief second it's like my brain has glitched. She's said the wrong thing. She's reading from the wrong script. I'm in the wrong story.

"My dad was involved in some shady business with Mr. Maxwell," she goes on. "It was ugly, bribes and blackmail, and it gets worse. Maxwell wanted my dad to push certain bills through the Senate to open up new oil drilling that the Maxwell company could exploit. There was a journalist who heard about some alleged kickbacks and was investigating it all, ready to blow the whistle. The entire thing was about to blow up, but then the journalist died in a plane crash. People might have believed it was just an accident, except your dad found the crash site and recovered the black box. If he'd gone to the authorities with it, they would have known the plane was sabotaged. So your dad had to be silenced to keep everything hidden."

# CHAPTER 16

MY ENTIRE BODY IS trembling as I clutch my cell. I replay everything Manderley just told me, then I recite to myself everything I know about my father. My dad was a paranoid schizophrenic who shunned modern technology and refused doctors and Western medicine. One day, his illness drove him past the point of no return. He burned down his cabin then hanged himself, so far back in the woods, so alone and secluded, that his corpse wasn't found for weeks.

That's what really happened. Not this ridiculous story Manderley made up about an assassination to hide the corruption between Senator Danvers and James' dad.

Her lies are even more insane than every single one of the delusions my father bought into combined. But why is she telling me all this? Has she grown crazy as well? Or is this just her desperate way to try to steal my fiancé back?

"Manderley," I say, trying to sound stern, "my dad was extremely mentally ill. He'd been that way for years. He was totally delusional, and if he really did come across a plane crash, he was paranoid and mistrustful enough he wouldn't have reported it to the government or the police or anyone else anyway."

"They weren't willing to risk it," she answers. "Not in an election year."

I shake my head at the absurdity of it all. "This is your father you're talking about," I remind her. "And you're telling me he murdered some random journalist and then killed my dad to cover that up?"

"The Maxwells were the ones who arranged for the plane to crash." Manderley's voice is slow. Expressionless. But there's something behind the words ...

No, she's lying and manipulative and maybe even crazy like my dad. I need to hang up and forget this conversation ever took place.

"I'm sorry you have to find out this way," she says. "That's why ... well, I couldn't let James know that I knew. That's why I put distance between myself and him, why ..." Her voice drops. "That's why I called off the engagement."

There's something in her words that clangs around and rattles in my head. *That's why* I *called off the engagement,* as if it were her choice and her choice only. I always pictured it as an agreement she and James arrived at mutually, but had he ever told me that specifically?

If she was the one who dumped him, what did that mean? That he would have rather spent his life with her and I'm just the consolation bride? That he was jilted, practically left standing at the altar, and I'm the second choice he had to settle for?

I need to get more information. I need to ask Manderley how she knows all this, for one thing. Does she have any proof, or is it her word against everyone else's?

And there's another question I can't understand. Even if Manderley is crazy enough to believe it's all true, why would she let me know? This information would ruin her entire family if it came to light.

"Listen," she says before I can formulate my next thought, "I know it's a lot to take in. But Clark's been working on this whole thing for over a year. It was his friend and mentor who was killed in that plane crash. We're trying to put enough pieces together to expose the whole truth, to let people know everything the Maxwells did."

"The Maxwells and your father," I add.

There's a pause. "Right," Manderley finally concedes. "And my father."

There are so many questions I need answered. Like when she mentions the Maxwells, who exactly does she mean? James' dad? His business?

The entire family?

"Is James part of this?" I can't believe I'm actually asking the question, can't believe I might possibly be entertaining the idea that Manderley is correct. Am I as paranoid as my father? Are we all living inside some type of shared delusion?

"I don't think so," she answers, "at least not directly, but he is now that you're in the picture."

I can't even begin to guess what Manderley might mean.

"You won't like what I'm about to say," she goes on, "but the whole thing was a setup, your engagement, him meeting you at the diner."

Immediately my mind flashes to the vicious rumors, the lies my coworkers told about James' mother paying the hostess to seat him at my table. I always assumed it was the jealousy of small-minded individuals who couldn't believe that two people from such vastly different backgrounds could meet and fall in love on their own.

"That's insane," I tell her. "If what you're saying really is true, there's no way the Maxwells would want me associated with their son."

"Unless they're trying to buy your silence."

The arguments all die in my throat as I think back to the prenuptial agreement, the document stating, amongst other things, that I would never speak publicly about my father to anyone.

"Have they asked you to sign anything?" she asks. "If you did, I'd bet my entire trust fund it included an NDA about your father, right?"

I'm dizzy. I feel as disoriented as my mom acted on days when she forgot who I was, couldn't figure out why I was living in her home or cooking in her kitchen. I don't know what's real and what's not, what's a lie and what's the truth. I want to ignore everything Manderley has said, want to toss it into a neat little garbage bag and forget we ever spoke. She's a jealous ex-girlfriend making one last pathetic attempt to ruin my engagement.

But what if she's right?

"I know this sounds crazy," Manderley says. "Clark and I didn't put all the pieces together until we did a little digging and discovered who you were, who your father was. And then it all made sense. Why his mother would have tried to set the two of you up. I know the Maxwell family. I know what they're capable of. And between you and me, I don't even want to know how deep all this goes. It's information that could get a lot more people hurt."

*Hurt.* Once she speaks the word, I replay it in my head. There's something menacing in her tone. Is Manderley Danvers threatening me?

My phone buzzes, and I'm so startled I nearly scream.

*Everything ok?* James is texting. *Mom just asked where you were.*

*Back in a few*, I type back as hastily as I can, given the shaking in my fingers.

"Listen," I tell Manderley, "I've got to go. All this is ..."

"If you don't believe me, ask Phillipa," she interrupts. "She's the one who told me and Clark about the diner, how Mrs. Maxwell made sure James would notice you. Start there. She'll confirm it."

My mind is racing, but before I can ask Manderley anything else, another incoming message makes me almost drop my phone.

*Coming?* It's James.

"Manderley, I can't talk to you anymore."

"Ask Phillipa," she urges. "And fast. Clark's trying to convince her to get back to the Philippines as soon as possible. If the Maxwells ever find out that she's been talking to us ..."

"I've got to go," I interrupt.

"Ask Phillipa," she repeats with pleading in her voice before I end the call, my breath choppy, my brain desperately trying to shake off the words I've just heard.

I have to get back. James is my fiancé, the love of my life. I know him, and I know his family. They would never do the things she's accusing them of.

Would they?

Manderley's some deranged ex-girlfriend with a grudge and an overactive imagination, that's all. Well, I won't listen to her. I'm not about to take a five-minute phone call with a deluded stranger and start questioning everything I know about James and his entire family.

The stuff about the diner is ridiculous. Probably Clark or Manderley overheard the jealous rumors from the other staff. And my father having incriminating information and stumbling across a black box from a plane crash?

Manderley is more insane than he was.

I bite my lip and clench every muscle in my body, trying to ignore the way I'm shivering. Now that the conversation has ended, I have a clear picture of exactly what I'm going to do. I'm going to forget Manderley Danvers ever called, ever spoke to me. I'm going to plaster on a smile and return to my future in-laws' home and mingle with their fancy, important guests. In a little over a year, I'll be Mrs. Daphne Maxwell, and Mrs. Daphne Maxwell would never appear rude at a dinner party or let a stupid prank call from some confused, unstable woman throw her off kilter.

I straighten my spine, resolve to become a woman worthy of James' name, and head back inside.

# CHAPTER 17

THE MOMENT I STEP into the Maxwell living room, my ears are assaulted with the sound of a dozen conversations taking place at once. The cacophony is a welcome distraction to my own racing thoughts.

"Oh, there she is." Mrs. Maxwell is making her way toward me, crystal glass in hand. She's smiling warmly, and I chide myself for even listening to Manderley's story for as long as I did. Of course it's nonsense. Yes, James' mother intimidates me sometimes, but that hardly means she forced her son to fall in love with me in order to cover up a murder. Besides, just because he was seated at my table didn't guarantee we'd end up engaged.

Unless James was also in on the plan ...

Before I know it, Mrs. Maxwell has slipped her arm around my waist and is raising her goblet. I ignore each and every one of the nagging doubts that are crawling inside my skin like hundreds of buzzing mosquitoes.

"I'd like to offer a toast," Mrs. Maxwell says, and silence falls on the room. "I want to give James and his bride-to-be my formal congratulations." She turns to look at me, and her smile is genuine, not the smile of a conniving killer. "Daphne, my dear, we are so thankful for the happiness you bring to our son and for this chance we have to welcome you into our family."

Her words are met with subdued applause and raised glasses. I have no idea where I'm supposed to look. I toss an awkward glance toward the kitchen and see Phillipa at the doorway. She hurriedly lowers her gaze and slips around the corner, out of sight.

"And now, one more happy announcement." Mrs. Maxwell unwinds her arm from around me and gestures to James' older brother. I'm relieved that the attention has turned away from me. My breath comes in short bursts like I've just completed a race.

I don't know Jefferson well at all. I've only met him long enough to form the opinion that I don't like him. He takes a step forward, his arm wrapped around his wife's waist just like Mrs. Maxwell's had been around mine. His glass is in the air, and I'm expecting something like a pregnancy announcement, except what he says is, "Well, it's official now and will be in the news by tomorrow at the latest. I've put my name in for the gubernatorial election next fall."

The room erupts in applause, only this time it feels actually genuine. James is standing next to me, and I think I sense his body tense, but I can't be too sure. Everyone is circling around Jefferson and his wife, everyone but James and me.

"Come on," he whispers. "Let's say our congratulations, otherwise I'll be hearing about it for weeks."

As we step up to the throng of people surrounding James' brother, I see Phillipa in the kitchen eyeing me warily. The moment our eyes meet, she slips back around the corner. Before I have time to make any sort of conscious decision or plan, I scurry after her. Everyone's so caught up in the election announcement I don't worry about being noticed.

Even though my legs seemed to follow me in here without the consent of my brain, now that we're standing together alone in the kitchen I know what I have to do. Not because I'm paranoid. Not because I trust anything Manderley Danvers said.

But because I want to put my mind at rest for good.

"Phillipa?"

She turns and looks as frightened as if I were coming after her with a gun.

"Phillipa, I just have a question I want to ask you. It's about Manderley Danvers."

Phillipa glances at the door, as if looking for someone to come in and rescue her.

"Please," I beg. "Manderley called me. She told me that this whole thing is a setup — meeting James at the restaurant, the engagement. She said I should ask you if I didn't believe her, that you could ..."

I such in my breath when one of the unnamed guests saunters into the kitchen.

"Whoops," he says when he sees the two of us. "I was just hoping to get a little more ice." He holds up his glass to Phillipa, and without saying a word or looking at me even once, she goes and fills it for him.

Separated now by space and a gargantuan marble countertop, I sense that Phillipa's not going to cooperate, even when we're alone again. She's not going to tell me anything. So what does that mean? If Manderley was lying, it would only take a single word. A simple denial.

Even a confused look, like she has no idea what I'm talking about.

A sickening feeling settles in the pit of my gut, and I realize that Phillipa's silence is almost as condemning as verbal confirmation. I step closer to her, but she shakes her head subtly.

*No.* What does that mean? No, Manderley isn't telling the truth? No, Phillipa can't talk to me now? Ever? What?

I remind myself of my conversation with Phillipa earlier in the day upstairs, when we were in the closet together and she was telling me about her sisters and family back home.

"Please." I keep my voice low, even though the din in the next room tells me that's not necessary. "Listen, you know about my family. My mom's in the nursing home. My dad's dead. James is all I have. And if our engagement is a setup …"

My voice catches. I'm not embarrassed for Phillipa to see me cry, but I'm afraid she'll think it's forced, that my tears are fabricated in order to manipulate her into complying.

I catch my breath and straighten my spine. I won't cry, and I won't beg. I'm giving Phillipa one chance to either confirm the lies that Manderley Danvers told me over the phone, and then I'm forgetting all about it. James' ex-girlfriend is jealous, unstable, and possibly even unsafe. There's no reason I should trust the words of a stranger over the love of the man I'm marrying.

I watch, my breath suspended in my lungs, as Phillipa's lip quivers. Then she shakes her head once more, ever so slightly, hardly even perceptible, and she scurries out of the kitchen as if running for her very life.

# CHAPTER 18

"Daphne! There you are!" Mrs. Maxwell's high-pitched greeting is so startling I clench my jaw to keep from gasping out loud. She's standing right in front of me, so close I feel her breath on my face. Or maybe I'm exaggerating. Sometimes with a brain like mine, it's hard to tell.

I hope I don't look guilty, that she won't see right through me, and I force a smile. "Oh." My subconscious mind has been working on a reasonable explanation, and I find myself casually stating, "I was just looking for a glass of water."

Mrs. Maxwell stares at me, one eyebrow raised slightly. "Of course, you need to ask the staff if there's anything at all you need. Remember, you're not a waitress anymore." She's smiling. On the surface, her words are as well-meaning as she ever is. Am I just imagining an undercurrent of derision?

I've never fully understood Mrs. Maxwell, but I always assumed that was because we were from different social circles. I think back to the phone call on the deck. Would someone like Beatrice Maxwell deliberately set me up with her son just so I'd sign a piece of paper? To think that

Mrs. Maxwell purposely dangled her son in front of me like a prize so I'd do whatever it was she asked ...

I stare at her for a moment, surprised that I'm even entertaining the idea.

If his mother could mastermind a plot so elaborate, was James in on it too? I think back to the prenup he and I signed less than an hour ago. That last clause about not speaking to the press about my father. It's not as if I've ever done anything like that in the past. Not as if I would have considered doing so at all. Is that the only reason James asked me to marry him? So I'd sign a piece of paper? I remember something Logan said about the non-disparagement clauses and assume it remains in effect whether we stay together or not. Is it possible he never had any real intentions of marrying me, but just goaded me on to buy my silence?

No. That doesn't make sense. James wouldn't do that.

But his mother ...

Mrs. Maxwell hasn't taken her eyes off me. "Daphne?" she asks, her voice dripping with concern. "Are you all right? You look a bit unwell, dear. Here." She steps past me, opens a cupboard, and pulls down a goblet. She fills it with water from the fridge and forces it into my hand. "It's rather warm tonight, isn't it? And so many people in there. It can be terribly stuffy at times."

Her smile is genuine. Her words are natural and easy. I take the water she offers and gulp down the entire thing. Mrs. Maxwell is right. It's hot out. It's more people than I'm used to being around. And I'm on edge because of that call from my fiancé's jealous ex, who's desperate enough to stoop to whatever lows she has to in order to break us up.

That's all this is. I let out my breath, feeling the tension and stress and fear excrete from my lungs. I know now that I have nothing to worry about, absolutely nothing at all. I'm probably on edge as much about the gathering of strangers as I am about Manderley's call. Five years from now, this type of get-together will feel totally normal to me. Maybe this is how James and I will make our first pregnancy announcement to the sounds of cheers and congratulations and clinking glasses. And Mrs. Maxwell will hand me a water goblet, reminding me that an expectant mother needs to stay hydrated. We'll share a smile, and for a split second I'll remember how she used to intimidate me, how at one point in my early engagement I was so insecure in James' love for me, so uncertain of my place in his family, that I actually entertained some crazy idea I heard from a deranged Manderley Danvers and let it throw off my equilibrium.

Maybe at that point I'll be close enough to Mrs. Maxwell I'll even mention tonight's phone call to her. "Beatrice," I'll say, with this carefree manner I will have picked up by then, "did I ever tell you about how James' old ex called me when we were engaged and what she tried to get me to believe?" And Beatrice and I will share a laugh, joking about the past until James comes in to escort me back to the happy gathering of friends who want to congratulate us on our good news.

"Babe, you in here?" James' words snap me back into the present. I glance at his mother, embarrassed that she might have seen my expression and deciphered my daydreams, but she's not looking at me.

"Daphne was a little thirsty," she tells her son, her voice as calm and as normal as if I've been in her family for years. "I was telling her it's such a hot summer." She turns back toward the living room, but as she passes, she gives me one last glance. "Do feel free to go up to the balcony later if you need a little fresh air."

James is staring at me quizzically. I eye my water glass and give him what I hope is a reassuring smile. "You okay?" he asks.

"Of course." I take his arm, as casually as I imagine it will feel years from now when tonight is nothing but a distant memory, and we return to the party.

# CHAPTER 19

WHEN I'M BACK IN the crowded room with all the guests, I do my best to pretend as if I'm happy to be there. I do my best to pretend as if my entire world hasn't been threatened with an extinction-level event.

James and his mother, conspiring to keep me silent about my dad?

I run through everything Manderley told me, everything she thought I'd be gullible enough to believe. How many coincidences would have to have lined up for it to go even remotely as she suggested?

First, Senator Danvers and Mr. Maxwell were involved in shady business. That's easy enough to believe, I suppose. But then to think that they'd sabotage a plane, kill an investigator before he leaked the story, and after that it just happened to be my father who stumbled across the rubble and found the black box ...

My dad hated technology, thought that anything with a Wi-Fi signal could cause cancer or lead to mind control or make you infertile or maybe all three. Would he have even known what a black box was for? I have no idea what it looks like. Maybe it was like his ham radio, something he could understand after all.

Still, if Manderley's delusions are correct, that means that my dad found the crash site, understood enough about the evidence to grow even more assured about some government plot, and then Danvers or Maxwell or somebody in their circle killed him, burned down his cabin, and staged the scene to look like suicide. Surely before murdering him they would have found out my dad was raving mad. This man who'd been muttering for years about UFOs and weather balloons deliberately poisoning the oceans and mind control devices in internet signals ... he wasn't a threat at all. Even if every single thing about the plane and the corruption and the coverup was true, my father couldn't have acted as a whistleblower.

Nobody would have believed him.

Unless he still had the black box in his possession, tangible proof that that plane had been tampered with to murder the journalist. Is that why the cabin was burned? My dad loved the woods he lived in as much as he hated new technology. It always seemed strange to me that he burned down his cabin before he died, since he of all people would have known the risks of starting a forest fire.

Actually, the fact that the cabin burned and the fire died out so quickly afterward did seem a little odd. Easier explained if the person who started the fire was there to keep it contained after my father was dead ...

Now I'm sounding as insane as he was. Instead of worrying about inheriting my mother's genes, maybe I should have been more concerned about my father's. At what age does schizophrenia show itself in women? Late twenties? Early thirties?

In other words, if I was cursed with my father's illness, isn't now the exact time it'd start to show up? For as many hours of my life as I've spent anxious about Alzheimer's, I've never once considered until just now the possibility of inheriting my father's disease.

James gives my hand a squeeze, and I force my mind to the present, force myself to laugh at the joke his brother's just told, something about elections and Washington and dead voters casting more ballots than the living. Doesn't that sound a little paranoid too? Don't we all entertain a few beliefs that would sound crazy to an outsider?

To someone sane?

"Excuse me, Daphne, I think you dropped your napkin."

Before I can respond, Phillipa has thrust a piece of cloth into my hand. Her eyes catch mine for a fraction of a second before she looks away, and in my palm I feel something in addition to the fabric. What is it? My eyes dart around the room, looking for Mrs. Maxwell, but she must have stepped out for the moment.

"Thank you, Phillipa." I keep my voice as calm as possible as I maneuver a piece of wadded paper from the napkin to my sweaty palm then shove it into the pocket of my pants.

The next few minutes pass like an eternity as I wait for the right moment to excuse myself. It has to look natural, and enough time has to pass after my exchange with Phillipa that people won't become suspicious.

Immediately, my mind darts back to my father, to the way he taught me to sneak about, the booby traps he instructed me how to make that last summer I spent with him.

*In case anybody finds out what we're doing.* I was young enough that it felt as much like a fun, playful adventure as preparing rabbit snares for the winter or seeing who could catch the biggest trout in the lake. It wasn't until Mom came that August to pick me up, until I saw her reaction to my father's ramblings, that I started to wonder if something was actually wrong.

"So your father said you dug a shelter?" she pressed gently on the long drive home to Anchorage. And in my naivete I told her all about the bunker we dug and how we stocked it with food and supplies in case the bad guys came and told Dad he couldn't stay on the land anymore.

To her credit, Mom did her best to keep her voice casual, her tone light as she questioned me more. "What bad guys would ever bother your dad about where he lives?"

And I told her all about the Feds and how the government guys were mad because Dad knew all about their secret weapons stash out in the woods and they made him promise not to tell anybody about it. But he knew that one day they'd come after him, and that's why we were digging out the bunker.

A week later, I was repeating this story to the school counselor, after that a social worker.

From then on, visits to my father were shorter, in public settings like the Eureka Lodge, and Mom was always there with me. My childhood summers in the woods, living off the land so far removed from anybody else, had come to an end. But this was years before Danvers became a Senator, years before that plane crash killed that journalist.

In other words, my dad was always ranting about corruption and coverups.

Is it possible that one of his conspiracies was actually true?

"You okay?" James asks when I stand up. I don't know if enough time has passed. I don't know if I look casual enough to avoid arousing suspicion. All I know is I need to find someplace private so I can look at the note that's burning against the fabric of my pocket.

"Yeah," I reassure him. I lower my voice, even though the guests are all absorbed in some story James' brother is relating. "Just need to go to the bathroom," I explain.

Once inside the restroom, with the door locked behind me, I pull out Phillipa's note with shaking hands. Her handwriting is small and feminine and unobtrusive. She's jotted down a phone number with an area code I don't recognize, and beneath that a single sentence.

*Call after 10 pm.*

# CHAPTER 20

I STARE AT THE note again. More secrets to unravel?

*Call after 10 pm.* She couldn't have given a single hint? Couldn't have written something like, *Daphne, your future mother-in-law is implicated in the murder of at least two innocent people and your entire engagement is a farce. Run away.*

But it means something's going on, doesn't it?

*Call after 10 pm.*

If it was nothing at all, if everything Manderley told me was completely unfounded, Phillipa would have denied it or ignored it completely. Not gone through some type of secret-spy song and dance to hand me a cryptic message. I'm surprised it wasn't written in invisible ink or on some type of self-destructive paper.

I think about everything I know about Phillipa, which aside from a few details about her family in the Philippines is basically nothing.

*Call after 10 pm.*

It must mean that something Manderley said is true. Doesn't it have to? But it all sounds so absurd. A journalist assassinated, my father murdered. If any of this was real it'd cause the biggest scandal in the entire state of Alaska.

Even the lies about the diner were silly. Mrs. Maxwell had nothing to do with me meeting James there. It was God's hand that brought us together, not some elaborate hoax meant to buy my silence.

*Call after 10 pm.* I don't know what Phillipa's up to. I don't know if this is her phone number or someone else's. I don't even know yet if I'm going to call tonight or not.

But I do know this. James is my soulmate. He is an upstanding, godly man, a pastor. Even if there's the smallest percentage of a chance that his family's involved in illegal activity, James isn't part of it.

And he didn't deliberately woo me and propose to me just so I'd sign a stupid piece of paper. Besides, what would be the point? And when would it end? Would we simply stay married for decades and have babies and build a life together, and the entire time it's nothing but a farce to keep me from telling anybody about my dad?

Manderley has been bitter about James for years. Of course she'd make up any lie she could about our engagement. That's what this is.

Ridiculous.

*You know who you sound like, don't you?* I shove the thought as far down into the recesses of my mind as possible, but it still lingers there, ready to pounce the second I turn my attention away from it. *You sound delusional. You sound crazy.*

*You sound just like your dad.*

I'm shaking now, my whole body a trembling mess of stress and fear and confusion.

I feel the constriction in my lungs. The state I'm in, I could turn into a crying, blubbering, panicking mess any moment. *God,* I pray, *I really need your help.*

He answers me in the form of a phone call from Gus at the nursing home. I suppose if anything could snap me out of my hysterics, an emergency involving my mother would do the trick.

"Gus, is everything okay?" I don't bother trying to hide the terror in my voice.

"Yeah, yeah, it's fine. Sorry, did I scare you?" Gus's voice is strong. Normal. Comforting.

I let out a sigh. "You have no idea."

"Did I catch you at a bad time?" he asks. "Are you in the middle of something?"

I try to force a laugh. "Oh, you know, just sitting here wondering if I'm losing my mind and going crazy."

"Daphne," he says, "you're one of the most sane and stable and caring people I know. You're a devoted daughter, and you're getting ready to marry the man of your dreams. Is that what's going on? Wedding nerves? Remember everything I told you that went down when my sister was engaged? Woo-whee."

As Gus talks on in his calming way, I feel even more of my body begin to relax. The sob I was nearly choking on slides back down my throat, and my breath comes easier.

"Thanks," I reply. "I'm just ... anyway, you caught me spiraling. Is everything okay there? Mom's all right?"

"She's better than all right, Daphne. She just had a shower, we got her dressed and ready for bed, and, well ... Hold on. Let me put you on speaker. You'll want to hear this."

The tears fall the moment I realize what's happening on the other line.

*Amazing grace, how sweet the sound that saves a wretch like me.*

"You hear that?" Gus asks. His voice is brimming with joy and pride and love.

*I once was lost, but now I'm found. Was blind but now I see.*

This time I don't try to choke down my sob. "Gus, you have no idea how long it's been since I've heard her singing. You have no idea ... I've missed this so much."

"I know." Gus keeps his voice low so I can hear the ringing of my mom's voice in the background.

*Through many dangers, toils and snares I have already come.*

For a moment I've forgotten about Manderley and my father and dead journalists and my fears for my own mental health. I'm back at my childhood home in Anchorage while Mama sings to the Lord.

*'Tis grace that brought me safe thus far, and grace will lead me home.*

# CHAPTER 21

My mother's song has soothed me, or at least alleviated the worst of my panic. By the time I'm calmed down and ready to face the Maxwell clan again, I feel like at least I've snapped out of the downward spiral of anxiety and fear. This party has to be wrapping up soon. At ten, I can call the number Phillipa gave me to get more information. Until then, at least I have my mother's song to comfort me.

I'm thankful that James's brother has announced his run for governor, thankful that now the attention for the rest of the evening won't have to rest on me.

Except when I step back into the living room, it's as if I've walked into a sauna of hostility and tension. Every eye rests on me, even James' father, who I've never been fully convinced would recognize me if we bumped into each other at the grocery store.

They know. They know about the phone call, about Manderley Danvers, about everything. Phillipa told them, and now they're incensed that I would even question their family, doubt their integrity. The echo of my mother's voice in my mind grows fainter, but I still cling to the words. *The Lord has promised good to me ...*

I search out my fiancé, but James is staring at his phone and won't make eye contact.

"Sorry," I stammer. "I was just ..." What am I supposed to say next? Panicking because everything I know about my relationship with James and this family is based on duplicity? Terrified that I'm losing my mind, just like my mother ... or even my dad?

Mrs. Maxwell is the one who steps up and holds out her cell phone with my picture blown up on the screen. "I take it you haven't heard yet?"

Heard what? I have no idea what's going on. And why is my photograph on the *Anchorage Daily News* website again?

James is beside me now, his presence still a comfort if somewhat of a belated gesture. "Mom, it's not her fault."

I feel just like I did when I was a kid and social workers were interrogating me about my dad, bombarding me with questions that inexplicably made me feel ashamed, complicit in something I didn't understand. I'm confused and scared and for the most bizarre moment all I can think about is that time one summer when I saw an owl fly by carrying a small, writhing rabbit in its talons.

Chaos swirls around in my brain. I look to James, hoping he'll offer me some explanation.

"*Anchorage Daily News* figured out who your dad is." His voice has no emotion in it. No emotion whatsoever. The punch to my gut I expect to feel doesn't come. Perhaps I've used up my quota of surprise for the day. Either that, or maybe having an embarrassing fact about you printed up for everyone to see means very little when your entire life is collapsing around you.

Everyone in the room still stares at me, and I realize they're waiting for my reaction. What do they want me to do? Drop to my knees and beg forgiveness for having a mentally ill father? Instead, all I ask is, "How'd they find out?"

Mrs. Maxwell shoves her phone in front of my face, even though my mind is so foggy I can't focus on the words on her screen. "They say that their reporters confirmed it. That *you* confirmed it." Her eyes narrow, and I feel James put a protective arm around my waist.

"I never talked to any reporters." It's all I can think to say. I look to James. Is he mad at me? Embarrassed now that the world knows who I am? What about that stupid non-disclosure clause I signed? Will I get in trouble now that the truth is out?

"Apparently you did talk to a reporter." Mrs. Maxwell clears her throat and holds her phone closer to her face while she reads from the article. "*Daphne Winters confirmed with an* Anchorage Daily News *reporter that she is the daughter of Frank Chilkoot. Chilkoot lived near Eureka and claimed to have damning evidence against the Maxwell family before his untimely death, which at the time was ruled a suicide.*"

"It's a lie, I never ..." My voice and my feeble protest both die in my throat, and I remember the coffee shop.

Clark.

Manderley Danvers is behind this. There's no other explanation.

"I saw someone at Kaladi Brothers ..." I don't even know where to begin. Clark. Manderley. My father. I can't get my words straight, can't hold onto a coherent thought long enough to defend myself. Suddenly I feel dizzy, and I'm thankful that James is here to hold me up while his entire family eyes me with open hostility.

"Look," James says, "this is all getting blown way out of proportion. What happened with Daphne's dad was years ago. The tabloids will talk for a day or two, then they'll forget about it, and life will all go back to normal."

Mrs. Maxwell doesn't look at either of us. "It had better." Her words cut like a metal blade chopping through the thickest of ice.

# CHAPTER 22

FASTER THAN AN AVALANCHE can leave wreckage in its wake, each and every guest has cleared out, shuffling away with pathetic excuses or embarrassed apologies for leaving early. James' father and brother have left for a meeting with the company's head of PR. Beatrice Maxwell is on the phone berating the editor-in-chief of *Anchorage Daily News*, demanding a retraction and public apology.

It feels like entire days have passed since the report was published online. James hasn't returned to the living room since seeing the last of the guests off, and I can only imagine what he's doing now or what he's thinking. I glance at the time. It's less than an hour until ten, and the note with Phillipa's mysterious phone number is still wadded up in my pocket. Do I want to know what I'll learn if I call? I assumed it was Phillipa's number, but I have no way of knowing that for sure. Maybe it's something else entirely, an FBI tip line or some prerecorded secret message or one of those cell phones connected to a bomb that'll detonate the moment it rings. No, that's ridiculous. It's got to be Phillipa's number, and she doesn't want me to call until later, presumably when she'll be in her own room above the Maxwell garage and able to speak in safety and in private.

But still, it feels dangerous. A Pandora's box I don't want to open. Regardless of what really is going on with James and his family, I won't be able to rest until I've discovered the full truth. It's already too late for me to bury my head and pretend none of this is happening.

The box is already open.

I nearly jump when my cell phone rings.

"Becca," I breathe, and relief courses through me. I don't know how long I'll be able to keep the living room to myself, so I make my way out onto the balcony, thankful for the summer breeze that's helping snap my brain out of its hazardous spiraling.

"Daphne, what in the world is going on?" My roommate's voice on the other line is frantic. "There are reporters outside," she hisses. "The landlord's livid. I can't get them to go away, and when they come to the door, they just ask for you. Are you in trouble? Is it about the engagement announcement or ..."

I sigh. "It's my dad. The press found out who he is."

I glance into the Maxwell home. The living room is still empty. Has everyone left? Even Phillipa? And where is James? Why is he taking so long?

"That doesn't make sense," Becca argues. She's one of the only people I've talked to openly about my father's history. "Not to sound calloused or anything, but who cares if your dad was mentally ill? I'd get the hype if he were some kind of child predator or even some Madoff-esque white-collar criminal. But from what you've told me, it sounds like he was just a sad, sick man. So what's with the paparazzi?"

I know the answer before she finishes asking the question, and the reality of it all settles in my gut like acid and curdles in my abdomen. "There's more to it than that," I tell my roommate. "I guess some people think he had dirt on the Maxwells and their business, and that's how he ..."

"Daphne?" James interrupts and steps out onto the balcony. "Mom just heard back from the Daily News. Can you come inside?" He glances at my phone as if seeing it for the first time. "Who are you talking to?"

"It's Becca," I answer before turning my attention back to my roommate. "Listen," I tell her, "I need to go, but I'll try to call you back soon."

"Don't bother," she says. "I've got to wake up at four in the morning, so I'm turning off my phone and gonna try to get some sleep. But if I were you I'd avoid coming home right away if you want to avoid the press. Eventually they'll have to get sick of waiting."

"Okay. I ..." I falter, unsure of what to add. *I'm sorry journalists are harassing you because my father was crazy.* Except was he crazy? Or was he actually telling everyone the truth?

"Try to get some rest," is all I say.

Back inside the Maxwells' living room, there's a strange electric buzz in the air, the leftover reverberations of all the noise and chaos that bombarded the condo walls all evening. But instead of family and friends and strangers, the only people in the room now are James and me, standing awkwardly in front of his mother, who's seated in an oversized armchair. I glance around but don't see Phillipa anywhere. Has she gone up home for the night?

"Well, Daphne," Mrs. Maxwell says with a tiredness in her voice I've never heard before. "It appears as though this so-called journalist you met today was recording your conversation, albeit without your consent. Unfortunately, that's not illegal in this state, and since you were in a public location we can't argue any sort of assumption of privacy. Does this sound at all familiar to you?" She presses a button and the audio recording sounds over the room's high-tech stereo surround system, replaying my conversation with Clark.

"Yeah," he's saying, "I grew up in Tolsona but moved here to Anchorage as soon as I could, and even that wasn't soon enough. I did some retail work, hated it, tried fast food, hated it even more. Once I turned 21 I started tending bars, which wasn't too bad, but now I'm working for *Anchorage Daily News*. Living the dream, right? At least the hours are better, and I don't have to call anybody a taxi home. Anyway, what is it you do for a living?"

Mrs. Maxwell stops the recording and stares at me.

"I mean, I didn't think ..." I have no idea what I'm saying and I'm thankful when James cuts in.

"He mentioned his work, but that's different than saying *Hi, I'm So and So, I'm a journalist for the* Anchorage Daily News *and would like to ask you a question on the record.*" I'm glad James is here to defend me, to put into one succinct sentence the paragraphs and pages of jumbled arguments that have been spiraling around in my brain.

Mrs. Maxwell lets out a sigh. "That's exactly what I told the attorney. Unfortunately, even if we were to argue the case in court, the story is already out there." She looks at me, but she doesn't seem angry like I would have expected. Just tired and resigned. "Daphne, I'm sorry this came out the way it did, but I don't hold you at all responsible." Her voice is full of compassion and concern.

"I hate to say it," she continues, "but the next few days might be unpleasant for you with journalists snooping around your business."

I mention that the press are already at my apartment.

"Well, if that's the case ..." Mrs. Maxwell stands up and gives me a sympathetic frown. "I've got a few more calls to make, but James, I want you to settle Daphne into the guest bedroom. She'll stay here for the night."

"That's not necessary," I start to argue, but James cuts in.

"Mom's right. If the press is hounding you about all this ..." He gestures vaguely. "I'll sleep better knowing you're safe from all that."

*Safe.* A dozen arguments are racing through my mind, but Mrs. Maxwell is already halfway upstairs. "It's settled then. I'm taking my calls in the office. Try to get some rest, and in the morning hopefully we can put this whole unfortunate business behind us."

All my protests die on my lips. I figure it's just as well. I'll have an easier time convincing James anyway.

"I don't want to be any trouble," I tell him. "I'd really prefer if you just took me home."

"With all the reporters?" James frowns.

Why did I even mention those reporters to him and his mom?

As I offer up another half-hearted protest, James leads me down the hall and into the guest room. The carpet is plush and impeccable, as if nobody's stepped on it for years. The walls are painted a rosy pink, and there are fake flowers on the dresser and on the nightstand.

All of a sudden I feel trapped, claustrophobic. I need to get out of here.

"It's been a long and hard day. I really want to sleep in my own bed tonight." I sidle up to my fiancé and wrap my arms around his waist. "Please? As a favor to me?" I pout my lips and stare up at him. He can never refuse me anything when I ask him like this.

Except tonight he does. James disentangles himself from me and takes a step toward the door. One sudden move and he could close it behind him, shutting me in here.

My stomach lurches. "What's wrong?"

"Nothing." His response is too fast. Too gruff.

"James," I plead, suddenly realizing how alone and defenseless I am. "You're making me nervous. What's going on?"

He shakes his head. "I just, I need some space. I need time to think."

Is he serious? James is the one who needs space? "What are you talking about?" I glance around this room I've never been in, a room that feels cold and empty and lifeless enough to trap me inside indefinitely.

"You never ..." James' voice is far too loud, and I flinch. He stops himself and closes the bedroom door before he begins again, this time in almost a hissing whisper. "You never told me who your dad was."

I sink onto the bed and stare at him, wondering if he's been replaced by some type of sentient AI that's very similar to my fiancé but not the real James Maxwell at all.

"What are you talking about?" I want to laugh, it's so ridiculous, but there's nothing funny about this conversation. Nothing at all. "I told you everything," I remind him. "I told you about our summers together, about the schizophrenia, how he burned down his cabin and ..." I don't want to complete that sentence, so I simply repeat, "I told you everything."

James is staring at me as if I'm as unknown to him as he is to me. "You never told me he was the one investigating my family." He's pacing the bedroom now, his feet trampling the immaculate carpet. Each time he moves it makes me wince. I shoot a glance at the door, wishing he'd kept it open.

"James ..."

His glare is full of venom. "Did you know who I was when you saw me at the diner? Is that why you were so flirty with me when we first met?"

His words sting more than a slap to the face. For several moments, neither of us speak. We simply stare at each other. I'd stand up and leave, but he's blocking my exit. And besides, he's the one who drove me here tonight. I have no way to get myself home, to safety.

Fear and anger and hurt and confusion all war for space in my mind so that I can only focus on one singular coherent thought.

*God, help me.*

# CHAPTER 23

THE SILENCE IS HEAVY and ominous. James' fists are clenched, and he speaks through a gritted jaw and asks me once more, taking special care to enunciate each word, "Did you know who I was when we met?"

I shake my head. "No. I didn't have any idea." I have to get him to believe me. I've never seen this type of anger in his eyes before.

"I'm not messing around with you. Manderley broke my heart once, and I'm never going through that pain again."

I can't show surprise when he names his ex. He always made me think their breakup was somewhat boring and uneventful, an inevitable thing that happened like a cold you catch and then move on. He's never mentioned a broken heart before, but I can't think about that now. I need to focus, and I need to get out of here.

He looks so angry and in need of solace that I want to take a step closer to him, out of habit if nothing else, but I stop myself. For the first time, I realize I have no idea who this man is, and as I stare at the way his chest is heaving

I'm reminded how unprotected and alone I am in this huge house.

Just me, James, and his mother.

*God, please get me out of here.* I don't know what else I'm supposed to pray, how I'm supposed to get James to trust me or at least allow me to leave.

"Listen, James." I try to keep my voice calm and soothing. "What came out in that news article was as much a shock to me as it was to you. Believe me, tonight's the first I've heard of any possible connection between my dad and yours. I promise you, I'm not making this up."

My whole body is trembling so hard it's a miracle my voice is steady enough to even speak.

I glance again at the bedroom door, begging and hoping for some form of escape. But then what? Once I'm out of this room, I'm still dependent on James for a ride home, but rage is contorting his entire demeanor, twisting him into something disfigured and dangerous before my eyes.

James throws his hands up in the air. "I can't believe you never told me your father was Frank Chilkoot. *Frank Chilkoot.*" He spits out the name like a curse.

"How was I to know the name would mean anything to you?" I feel like crying, not from sadness or even anger but out of sheer confusion. James has always been there to comfort me when emotions regarding either of my parents get the best of me, except now I don't even recognize the man I pledged to marry.

"That man ruined my life with his ridiculous allegations. He ruined my life, Daphne." He's pacing now, and I can almost feel the heat of his fury radiating off of him. I've never seen James so worked up. What happened to the kind and gentle man I once knew, the kind and gentle man I love?

"Please," I beg, "I had no idea. I don't even know what he did to you."

"He claimed he had proof that the Maxwell Oil Company was involved in some type of collusion. My father needed a fall guy, and it happened to be me. They fired me so that if we were ever investigated, I'd be the one to take the blame."

I stare at James, at how different this story is from all the times I've heard him talk about his call to ministry, his love for the pulpit, his disdain for the cutthroat environment of his family's business.

"Then, as if that wasn't enough to ruin my life," James goes on, "there was evidence of a kickback my father gave Senator Danvers, the kind of 'donation' that isn't exactly legal. It was an election year, and the fallout of that would have been horrific if the public got a whiff of it. The Danvers family had to distance themselves from us. That's why Manderley called off the wedding."

For a moment, what shocks me most isn't the dangerous rage emanating from this man I once knew, but the raw, wounded pain I see in his eyes when he mentions his breakup. And because there's so much inside me that loves this man, regardless of the fear in my gut, I want to go to him, to comfort him, to let him know that I understand what it's like to lose the most important people in your life.

James stops pacing and looks at me, and for a moment I think I see the tenderness that we've always shared with one another.

Then his expression hardens. “I thought I was over all that, thought it was all in the past, until it comes out in the press that your father is the same man who ruined my life. So I’m going to ask you again, Daphne. Did you know who I was when we met?”

This time, the tears threatening to spill over find their way to the corners of my eyes. “I didn’t have any clue,” I assure him. Mechanically, I’m trying to convince my fiancé how much I love him, but in the back of my mind runs one single, defining thought:

*James is still in love with Manderley.*

I steady my voice. “When we met, I was just a girl waiting tables at a diner. I wasn’t hiding anything from you. I told you about my father, and if I never mentioned his name it’s because I never thought it was important. So if you think I sought you out for some ulterior reason, that’s not how it happened at all. I love you, James.” As soon as I speak the words, I feel in my entire body how true they are, like a gong that reverberates with a sound so pure and unadulterated it sets your very soul vibrating. It reminds me of one of the Bible verses James himself used in his sermon just a few weeks ago: *The truth will set you free.*

“I fell in love with you on our very first date.” The words feel expansive in my chest, as they continue to resound with the loud clarity of truth. “I didn’t know who you were or who your family was or even why I felt so drawn to you. All I knew is I’d been looking for you, praying for you my entire life. I told myself it was just a crush, but I couldn’t get you out of my head, and when you came back and sat at my table the very next day, I felt like my legs would give out beneath me. From that first date on, I knew you were my soulmate. I love you more than anything else in this entire world, and I ..." My voice catches.

I see a softening in James' features, and I speak the next words slowly and carefully. "I guess it's time we both tell each other the full truth. I had no idea my dad was connected to your family, but obviously somebody did. And some people seem to believe that it wasn't God or chance or fate that set us up at all, but your mom."

James looks confused. "My mom?" he repeats, and I tell him about the rumor swirling around the diner, only leaving out the fact that it was Manderley Danvers who most recently repeated that information.

"I assumed people were just gossiping," I explain. "I never paid attention to it, but then when I heard about the connection between your dad and my dad ..."

I'm trying to figure out what I see in James' expression, but I can't name it. The unfiltered anger has dissipated, but I wouldn't exactly call this a look of love or gentleness either. James stands there as if stunned, like his body's connection to his brain has been cut off and now needs a few seconds to reset itself.

I wait until I fear the silence will drive me mad. But before I can ask him to talk to me, someone knocks outside the guest room. Like vapor escaping a steam room, the confusion vanishes from his face the moment Phillipa cracks open the door.

"Excuse me, James?" she says quietly. Her face gives no indication that she overheard any of our conversation, and she doesn't look at either of our faces, just at the space between us on the pristine cream carpet. "If you're not busy, your mother would like your help moving a box down from her things in the attic."

James blinks, and the moment he reopens his eyes he looks like himself again, or at least a tired and somewhat more burdened version of himself. He nods at Phillipa . "Okay."

Before I can say a word to either of them, Phillipa has turned away, and James is heading after her.

He stops to look back in the doorway and offers me one sad, almost apologetic glance — a look which contains more information than a hundred news articles.

This look tells me everything. James wasn't aware his mother paid to have him seated in my section. Not until tonight. But it's true. I should be thankful to discover that James wasn't in on the lie. We were both pawns in his mother's scheme. Which means that our relationship could recover from this blow, but only if it weren't for the soul-wrenching sadness in my fiancé's eyes.

James touches my hand as he exits the room, a soft brushing, the back of his finger against mine. There's nothing romantic in the gesture at all, but it's enough to speak a thousand words. A thousand apologies.

A thousand goodbyes.

# CHAPTER 24

MINUTES TICK BY WITH painful monotony. I'm left alone in this cold and comfortless spare room, wondering how much longer James will take. We have so much unfinished business to discuss.

I hear the sound of something being scraped across the floor above me. That must be the box she needed help with. I strain my ears but don't hear any voices. Does that mean James is almost done?

I refuse to pull out my phone, refuse to stumble across any news articles about me or notifications on my social media accounts. Instead I sit on the side of the bed.

Waiting.

It's late enough I could try to call Phillipa, but she was just here and might not be back to her own room yet. Besides, James could return any minute. Unless he went home without even checking on me or saying goodbye. Would he have done that? I've never seen him as angry as he'd been earlier. Then again, I've also never seen him looking as sad as he did when he left me alone in this sterile cell.

My body is exhausted but my mind keeps racing, and I can feel dozens of imaginary knots in my unbrushed hair. I need to get home. I need a shower and I need my own bed. Thinking of spending the entire night here without my brush makes my scalp itch like crazy, and I need some way to harness this nervous energy. Scratching will only make the tangles worse, so I pull up a thought of my mother when she was younger — calm, serene, beautiful. The mental imagery works, and I feel my entire soul relax slightly at the thought of Mom singing to me while she gently tames the knots in my hair, her breath so close to my ear I can almost smell the mint of her toothpaste.

*The Lord has promised good to me, his word my hope secures.*

Mom always had a beautiful voice, but she didn't like singing if strangers could hear her. That's what makes my memories of her music even more special. They were saved for moments when it was just the two of us.

*He will my shield and portion be as long as life endures.* Peace floods my body. My breath slows, and it's almost as if I can feel my mother's loving arms and tender prayers surrounding me, wrapping me up like a downy blanket on a cold winter day.

*Through many dangers, toils and snares I have already come*. I don't know where my fiancé is. I don't know what either of us are going to do now that the truth has come out about how we met, about who our parents are. But I do know that the words of Mom's song are as true today as they always have been and always will be:

*'Tis grace that brought me safe thus far, and grace will lead me home.*

I remember the miracle of hearing her singing on the phone when Gus called me earlier. I remember waking up this morning and spending time with my Bible journal, feeling so energized as the colors formed on the page. I remember playing with Jasper and taking him for a walk along the trail behind the parsonage this evening.

And then I remember the anger in James' voice when he accused me of knowing who he was before we met. The unhealed emotions in his face when he talked about Manderley breaking up with him so many years ago. The finality I felt in his parting gesture when he stepped out of the room ...

He's been gone for nearly twenty minutes. I glance out the window to see if I can spot his car, but the deck awning blocks the view down to the driveway. The summer sun still shines bright, leaving angular shadows on the guest room bed. It's been made up severely, and I picture Phillipa working in here, taming the sheets with sharp hospital corners, situating the pillows with impeccable austerity. I've seen dental chairs that look more warm and welcoming than this room.

I can't stay here anymore. I grab my phone and call James, but the call goes immediately to voicemail before I can beg him to take me home.

As I stare at the screen, I'm hit by an inexpressible urge to call my mom, but there's no point. She's probably asleep, and if she isn't, it's the time of day when she's likely to be the most confused. Either way I don't want to interrupt her. So instead I picture my mother as she was in the past. Anything to ignore the heaviness in my heart, as if my soul has already discovered something my conscious mind is not aware of yet.

"Mama," I ask her one afternoon. We're sitting at the kitchen table, tying little ribbons on lollipops for my school's Valentine's Day exchange. "What's a soulmate?"

"A soulmate?" Mom looks out the window at the gray winter sky. "A soulmate's kind of like a best friend, but usually romantic. Like two people who were made by God to be together."

"Like you and Daddy?" I ask, and her face gets sad.

It's the same look James gave me when he walked out of this room.

Something thuds upstairs, followed by the sound of a shriek.

A woman screams.

The room rumbles, almost like an earthquake.

Tossing aside thoughts of my mom or James or of anything other than getting myself to safety, I jump off the bed and fling open the guest room door.

But it's not an earthquake. It's something far more gruesome.

Phillipa is lying at the bottom of the stairs, her body twisted at an impossible angle, while a puddle of blood forms beneath her.

Outside her bedroom door, Mrs. Maxwell stands staring down at her. Then she shifts her eyes to mine and meets my gaze with a look of cold, calculating hatred.

# CHAPTER 25

"I HAVE NO IDEA what could have happened," Mrs. Maxwell is telling the man in uniform. I've lost track of time since the ambulance arrived, and I can't begin to guess how Beatrice is keeping her voice so calm. "She must have tripped on the stairs while she was cleaning up after the party."

Paramedics are on the ground level, tending to Phillipa and talking in hushed voices. While I stand on the second-floor landing, my eyes scan the entire house for James. I can't find him anywhere.

"It's possible she helped herself to some of our champagne and had a bit too much," Beatrice offers. All I can do is stare at Phillipa's twisted body, so unnaturally bent.

"Who all was in the house when she was injured?"

Beatrice shakes her head. "It was just the two of us. This is Daphne Winters, my son's fiancé. We'd had a small get-together this evening, but everyone else had gone home."

A paramedic has placed a neck brace around Phillipa and they're working to shuffle her onto a board to transport. I'm relieved she's out of her contorted position, and I hold my breath while I wait to see if she moves or makes any noise.

"And your son is ..." the officer prompts.

"James Maxwell." Mrs. Maxwell's voice is calm and nonplussed. "He left about twenty minutes before it happened. He was one of the last to leave."

Phillipa is wheeled out of the front door on a stretcher. The paramedics aren't running and shouting like they do on TV. Nobody's straddling her chest on the porch trying to start IVs or perform CPR. Is it a good sign they're not in more of a hurry?

Or is it the exact opposite?

The officer asks Mrs. Maxwell to show him the layout of the house, and as soon as they've stepped away I feel my whole body start to tremble, as if it had been waiting for this touch of privacy before completely breaking down. I stare at a smear of blood at the top of the stairs then shut my eyes before my vision travels over to the larger puddle at the bottom.

"Would you like me to get you something to drink?" The voice startles me, and I jump back into my shaken body.

"I'm sorry," a woman with long brown hair apologizes. "Officer Baker." She reaches out her arm, and I'm certain she can feel my clammy hand trembling in hers. She reaches into a bag she's carrying and hands me a plastic water bottle then asks me for my name before I even find my voice to thank her.

She scribbles in her notebook without looking up at me while the questions continue.

"And did you see what happened?"

"No." The ambulance wail pierces the silent night, and I can't help but picture the unnatural splay of Phillipa's body at the base of the stairs just a few moments earlier.

Officer Baker keeps her pen poised above her notepad, so I take in a deep breath, trying to draw energy and alertness into my brain. "I was in the guest room." I gesture down the hall to the open doorway. "I heard a scream, then it sounded like something falling. At first I thought it was an earthquake, so I came out here, and there she was at the bottom of the stairs."

I can't pry my eyes away from that horrid red stain.

"And were you the first person to see her there?"

In the entryway, another police officer is taking photographs. So many photographs.

"Were you the first person to find Phillipa after she fell?" Baker repeats the question, snapping me back to our conversation.

"No, Mrs. Maxwell was standing here when I came out of my room."

"And her bedroom is on the same level as yours?"

I glance up the stairs that lead to the third floor, and that's when I realize what feels so off. "No. She sleeps on the top level."

"But by the time you came out of your room, you say Mrs. Maxwell was here, on this landing? Can you show me where she was standing?"

I rack my brain. "Hold on, I can't quite remember. I was surprised by the scream and the noise, and then I came out and I saw Phillipa, and it felt at first like an earthquake ..." I shake my head. "I don't know."

"But you're certain ..." Here Officer Baker levels her gaze and stares intently into my eyes. "You're absolutely certain that Beatrice Maxwell was already standing here on this second-story landing when you came out of your room?"

It's a simple question, but now doubt fills every crevice of my exhausted mind. "I think so, but it all happened really fast. She was on the phone, I think. She was calling 911."

Just like the details of a dream vanish within the first few seconds of waking up, everything I saw or thought I saw on the landing vaporizes into an ethereal mist.

"Where was Mrs. Maxwell when you came out of your room?" Baker repeats.

"I wish I could remember," I reply, convinced I'm the least reliable witness she must ever have interviewed. Should I tell her my mother has early-onset Alzheimer's? Should I tell her there's a chance I've inherited her disease but I'm too scared to take the screening test to find out for sure?

I try to quiet my brain so I can relive each precise moment before the emergency crews arrived. "I was in the guest room. I heard a scream, then something thudding or crashing down the stairs. It felt like maybe an earthquake, so I came out here." I'm not telling her anything new. I pause, first looking around at my surroundings then squeezing my eyes shut as if that might bring memories back to my faulty brain. "Phillipa was the first thing I noticed. I guess the rest just blurred out of my mind. I'm sorry."

Baker sighs. "That's okay," she assures me. "Before the scream, you didn't hear anything? Conversation? Fighting?

Even something totally normal like someone walking up or down the stairs?"

I wish I had more to offer, but I simply shake my head. "I don't remember."

"And can you confirm who else was at home when the accident happened?"

"They'd had a party," I begin, "but most people left by nine or just after." I'm hoping she doesn't ask me to try to name everybody who attended. "Then it was me and James, my fiancé, Mrs. Maxwell's son. And Mrs. Maxwell was upstairs. She wanted James to help her move a box ..." My voice trails off when I see the frown on Baker's face.

"So James was also at home when this all occurred?"

"I ... um ..." I lower my voice and feel my face flush. "I'm not sure."

She looks at me quizzically, and I hasten to explain. "James and I were in the guest room talking. Then his mom asked him for help getting a box from the attic. He went up. I waited around but didn't see or hear from him. His phone went right to voicemail when I tried calling. And then I heard the scream, and ..."

Baker nods, sparing me the difficulty of reexplaining the entire accident again.

"So you can't tell me for sure if James was or wasn't at home when this young woman was injured?"

I realize I'm not painting a good alibi at all, but I've told her the truth. I pull out my cell. "Want me to try to call him again?"

She shakes her head. "That's okay." She turns a page in her notebook, and even though the questions venture off to other topics than my fiancé, I can't shake the nagging question pounding between my temples.

*Where is James?*

# CHAPTER 26

IT'S AT LEAST ANOTHER hour before Officer Baker and her colleagues finish their questioning, with a promise of more to follow in the morning. Mrs. Maxwell continues to assure everybody that the fall was a tragic accident, the result of Phillipa's drinking. For a brief moment, there's talk of covering the house in crime tape and locking everything down. At the suggestion, Mrs. Maxwell makes one phone call to her good friend, the district attorney, and almost immediately afterward the police leave the condo like sled dogs being punished with their tails between their legs.

I've tried calling James at least a dozen times. Is he mad at me and refusing to answer my call?

Has something happened to him?

Or is he involved in all of this somehow?

I don't want to stay here, but I can't get a hold of Becca, and I don't have anybody else I can call to ask for a ride.

Once Mrs. Maxwell is upstairs and everyone else has left, I lock myself in the guest room, even though I seriously doubt my nerves will quiet down enough to let me fall asleep.

Sitting with my back against the headrest of the king-sized bed, I go through everything Mrs. Maxwell told the officers about tonight. According to James's mother, she was in her room when she heard a scream, ran down to the second floor, and saw Phillipa at the bottom of the stairs with blood oozing out from a major gash in her head. I want to believe that this entire catastrophe was a terrible accident. But I've never seen Phillipa touch alcohol, and I can't imagine her drinking on the job like Beatrice implied. So how does a healthy young woman just lose her footing in a home she knows so well and injure herself so grievously?

I wish there was someone at the hospital with Phillipa, someone I could call and ask for updates, or at least a familiar face there so that when she wakes up she won't be alone. I think about the note she passed to me at the party, the phone call I was supposed to make.

Was Phillipa going to explain everything going on in the Maxwells' twisted family? Maybe Beatrice found out and she tried to silence Phillipa by pushing her down the stairs.

The idea seems to have at least some merit, but I can't trust myself. I have no idea if my suspicions make sense or if I'm just as delusional as my father was. To himself, he sounded completely sane as he rambled on about UFOs and government agents trying to steal his DNA in order to make an army of Frank Chilkoot clones. I need an objective third party.

James is out. Even if I could get a hold of him, I can't trust him. Not without more information. The thought that I might not be able to believe my own fiancé leaves me feeling alone and orphaned in this lavish guest room.

I've tried calling Becca. She'll tell me if I'm acting paranoid. But she notoriously leaves her phone on *do not disturb* for days on end, and tonight is no exception. Unless she's awake at this ungodly hour and staring directly at her cell, she won't notice my call or text.

If Mom was herself, I would talk to her. She would understand better than anybody. Hopefully, she's sleeping soundly and peacefully at Pioneer Peaks.

Pioneer Peaks. That's my answer. My fingers only hesitate for a couple seconds before I call the number.

"Hello?" His voice is groggy, but the sound of it brings such a rush of warm relief I'm certain I've made the right choice.

"Gus," I exclaim, "I'm so sorry to wake you up, but I really need someone to talk to. I don't want to sound overly dramatic, but it's kind of an emergency."

Ten minutes later, Gus has drunk a cup of coffee to wake himself up, and I've explained everything that's happened today, from Manderley's phone call to Phillipa's note and her spill down the Maxwell staircase.

"So do the police think that your fiancé's mom had something to do with the accident?"

I'm relieved that Gus is the first to suggest the possibility. It makes my own suspicions feel more valid. "I'm not sure. I guess I assumed so at first. Then the police came, and one of the officers started asking me a lot of questions, like where Beatrice was when I came out of my room, where she was standing, what she was doing, and I was so tired and confused I felt like my mind was playing all kinds of tricks on me."

"Well, if the police really suspected her they would have brought her down to the police station. And they definitely wouldn't have let her stay in her house overnight to get rid of whatever evidence she wanted to."

I adore Gus for his somewhat naïve view of Alaska politics.

"Don't forget, this is the Maxwell family. The moment they mentioned a crime scene she called the DA and sent the police away packing. She's not the type of woman you just bring down to the station to interview on a hunch."

"Right, I guess that makes sense." Gus sighs on the other end of the line. "But really, if the police did suspect that this Maxwell woman was involved somehow, they wouldn't have just left you alone in the house with a murderer."

If I had called Gus to talk me down from my paranoia, I had grossly mistaken his reaction.

"Don't talk like that," I tell him. "Phillipa's going to be fine, and she can clear things up at the hospital. She'll let the police know if it really was just an accident or something else."

"Right." Gus is quick to agree then explains somewhat sheepishly, "I probably just watch too many of those crime documentaries late at night when I'm trying to wind down from a swing shift."

"Yeah." I force out an awkward laugh. "Most likely, this was just a really awful accident." I wonder if Gus hears both the hopefulness and the doubt in my voice. I don't think I'm fooling either of us.

"Still ..." Gus hesitates before continuing. "You've got to admit the timing is a little strange."

Something in the pit of my stomach sinks. “What do you mean?”

“I mean, this all happens the same day your fiancé’s ex-girlfriend gets in touch with you, and the one person she claims can confirm what she’s saying about his family ends up in the hospital. If this was ten years ago and we were back in school, the exact word I’d use is that it sounds a tad sus.”

I give a mirthless chuckle. “You’re supposed to tell me everything is absolutely fine and there’s nothing at all to worry about.”

For a moment, Gus doesn’t respond. When the silence persists, I check my phone to make sure the call didn’t disconnect.

Finally, Gus speaks. “You know what? Tomorrow’s my day off, so I don’t have to be up early for work. I’m gonna swing by and pick you up. You can crash on my couch if you want, or I can take you back to your place, or we can go to IHOP and eat pancakes and drink weak coffee. But I don’t think you staying alone with that woman is the smartest choice given everything that’s happened. What did the officer say when you told them about that note the housekeeper gave you?”

My mind freezes for a moment, like a website’s 404 page.

“Daphne?” Gus repeats his question. “What did they say about the note?”

“I didn’t tell them.” The words sound as hollow as my own soul at the moment. “I didn’t mean to keep it from them,” I hurry to insist. “The officer kept asking where Beatrice was standing, and I couldn’t remember, and the paramedics were there, and I was worried about Phillipa, and I couldn't figure out what happened to James or where he went, and I didn't even think about the note. Besides, Mrs. Maxwell was there all night. I couldn't have mentioned it without her overhearing."

"I understand." Gus's voice is gentle. "And that explains why they're not more concerned for you right now. But when you put all the pieces together, it sounds like that Maxwell woman could have had a decent motive for wanting to shut the housekeeper up. So give me the address. I'm getting dressed right now then I'm on my way to get you."

Gus has had the privilege of half a night of sleep as well as a cup of coffee, but my brain is so sluggish I can hardly keep up with anything he's saying.

"The address," Gus repeats. "Where does the Maxwell family live?"

I think I hear a noise outside my door, and I glance again to make sure that it's locked. I don't care if it makes me look paranoid.

"Daphne?" Gus asks.

I turn the volume on my phone down to the lowest setting.

"Someone's at the door," I whisper.

"Daphne?" Mrs. Maxwell's voice is sickeningly sweet. "Daphne, the door's locked. Can you let me in, please? I just got an update about Phillipa."

I'm frozen in place, and I clutch the phone in my hand, my last lifeline to safety.

"Daphne?" Gus has lowered his voice, perhaps sensing that I'm here frozen in fear.

"It's Mrs. Maxwell," I whisper. "I need to go."

"No," Gus hisses. "Don't let her in. Pretend to be asleep or something, but keep your bedroom door locked."

"Daphne?" I hear the jingle of keys and run toward the ensuite, not that I have any idea what I'll do once I'm in there.

"I've got to go." I keep my voice as low as possible. "I'll call you back soon."

"No," Gus replies earnestly. "Daphne, whatever you do, don't hang up the phone."

I thrust the cell into my pocket and rush toward the door as it swings open. For a moment, Beatrice and I stare at one another without moving.

"Daphne?" She raises an eyebrow at me.

"Sorry," I stammer. "I was just using the bathroom."

Beatrice eyes me up and down, then gives a slight nod. "Well, come on down to the living room. I'm heating us up some tea. The police officer called, and I'm afraid it's bad news. The doctors did everything in their power, but Phillipa has passed away, God rest her poor soul."

# CHAPTER 27

I'M SURPRISED TO FIND Logan, the Maxwell attorney, already in the living room. She's wearing a tracksuit, and I wonder how much she's getting paid to work like this when just about everyone else in Anchorage is asleep.

Mrs. Maxwell pours tea for us both and tells her lawyer, "I'm certain the police will want to question us both again in the morning, especially in light of the recent developments regarding the patient's health." Her voice is flat, and she may as well be talking about a cold snap halfway across the globe for all the emotion she's showing while she mentions the death of her longtime household employee. "Obviously, we'll want to work with the police as swiftly as we can so they can see that this was nothing but a tragic accident."

Logan hasn't met my gaze, but instead she glances at Mrs. Maxwell.

"And of course," Beatrice continues, addressing me, "if you find yourself with any signs of PTSD or shock from the stress of this evening, we are more than willing to make our family therapist available to you at no extra charge."

Mrs. Maxwell's words make individual sense, but strung together I can hardly make them out. Family therapist? PTSD?

"So." Logan punctuates the word like someone who understands the power of a monosyllable, and she slides a piece of paper across the coffee table toward me. "This is the statement I've prepared. If it all looks good, you can sign it tonight, and that will make tomorrow's interviews nothing more than a formality."

The phrases on the typed page are just as convoluted as the words swarming around me in the fancy living room. *Alone in the guest bedroom … Heard a female scream and the sound of something falling … Had been drinking earlier in the evening, which possibly explains …*

My face flushes hot, and I know even without looking at her that Mrs. Maxwell is staring at me.

"Is there a problem, Daphne?" Her voice is strong as immovable granite, and mine sounds squeaky and weak in comparison.

"I wasn't sleeping when it happened. I was drowsy, but …"

"Well, that's easy enough to rectify." Beatrice picks up the paper and shoves it toward Logan. Then she levels her eyes directly at me. "Is there anything else?"

"I don't remember seeing Phillipa drinking anything."

Mrs. Maxwell waves a hand dismissively in the air. "The blood reports will answer that question. Really, we just want to help the police out as much as possible and clear up this terrible mess. I'll have Logan make up a new draft, and once you've signed it you're welcome to go back to bed. I assume you haven't slept yet. You look completely exhausted."

I don't know what to say, so I simply watch as the family attorney picks up the printed statement and walks out of the room.

"Your face is pale," Beatrice states flatly. "Are you unwell?"

Unwell? A woman I saw just a few hours ago is now dead, and we're talking about my complexion?

Mrs. Maxwell crosses her leg, still fully dressed. "I know that putting everything into legal terms like this might come across as unfeeling, but you'll understand one day. The last thing we need is that woman's family attempting to sue us for wrongful death or anything like that. And I didn't like to speak ill of the dead while Logan was listening, but I'm not even convinced Phillipa's fall was an accident."

My breath catches in my throat. "What do you mean?"

"Well, this wasn't common knowledge, but I suppose I'll have to tell the investigators in the morning. Phillipa was found to have purloined two scarves from my daughter's collection. When I found the items in her bag last night, I told her that after she finished cleaning up from the party, she was fired. I can't have hired help in my own home if I can't trust them."

"I offered her the scarves. I'm sorry," I rush to add, "but she was helping me go through Jillian's things, and I thought it would be a thoughtful gift. I told her that if she wanted she could take a few from what I had already chosen for myself." Why hadn't Phillipa said anything when Mrs. Maxwell confronted her? I could have cleared it all up. I could have explained ...

"Phillipa was a thief," Mrs. Maxwell huffs, "and when she realized her job was over and she had no future prospects, she drank herself silly and took a tumble down the stairs. Whether deliberately or not doesn't really matter. The autopsy will show she was inebriated, and the scarves are in the office where I confronted her about her dishonesty. Now all that's left is for you to sign the paperwork Logan is preparing, tell the police the same information in the morning when they ask, and we can put all this behind us."

She glances at the door, but Logan still hasn't appeared. Beatrice lowers her voice. "Between you and me, my dear, I never did like the way she looked at James when he was here with you. In a terrible way, she might have done the two of you a favor by taking her own life like that."

I try not to let her see me gasp. Mrs. Maxwell reaches out, and I involuntarily shudder when her clammy hand clasps mine.

"And just think," she croons. "The sooner all this is in the past, the more attention we can spend on planning your picture-perfect wedding." Her smile is unnaturally large, her lips distractingly puffy.

She gives my hand an unyielding squeeze. "I'm a firm believer in starting a marriage off on the right foot. I'm willing to do everything to ensure that you and James have the happy engagement and beautiful wedding you deserve."

# CHAPTER 28

By the time Logan returns with a new statement for me to sign, I'm so tired my body is rocking back and forth. Or maybe that's just my brain or my vision playing tricks on me. I can't be sure. All I know is I'm not thinking straight, and I shouldn't sign anything until I've gotten some sleep and found the chance to clear my head. I still haven't figured out why Mrs. Maxwell wants me to sign a statement now since the police will be interviewing me in just a few hours, but maybe it's like she said. Maybe this is normal behavior for families of the Maxwells' status, with fortunes like theirs they need to protect.

It's the kind of thing I never learned about, growing up raised alternatively by a financially struggling single mother and a father descending deeper each year into the black abyss of his mental illness. The words on the page make very little sense to me. Logan, still wearing her feathered hoop earrings, is patient as she tries to explain.

"You know," I finally admit, "I'm so exhausted. Would it be okay with you both if I took this to the guest room and slept on it until morning? I'm sure once I've had at least a little bit of rest I'll be thinking way more clearly so I know what I'm signing."

Logan doesn't look at me but glances at Mrs. Maxwell, who frowns and lets out a small grunt of disdain. "The police want your memories to be recorded as close to the time of the event as possible. If we wait until morning, that's hours where you could forget even the smallest detail that might prove to them that this entire tragedy was simply an unavoidable accident. That's why I asked Logan to come over here at this unconscionable hour, so we could spare you even more headaches with the police down the road."

With that, Mrs. Maxwell nods to her attorney and tells her, "Leave the paperwork here, why don't you? Daphne and I will talk it over, and we'll call if we have any further questions. Otherwise you can go home and try to get some rest."

While Logan gathers her things, Beatrice turns and offers me an unfeeling smile. "The sooner we get this all taken care of, the better."

If Logan says goodbye, I don't hear it. I can't remember the last time I've been this exhausted.

"Shall I make you some coffee, honey?" Beatrice's voice has turned sweet, and her term of endearment rattles around inside my confused and foggy brain. "Heaven knows I could use a cup myself."

Without waiting for an answer, Beatrice leaves me alone in my seat, where I try to make sense of this piece of paper in my hand. *Drinking at the party ... distressed about an uncomfortable confrontation with her employer ... increasingly belligerent as the night progressed ...*

None of this sounds like Phillipa's behavior, and none of it is true. How could I sign my name to something full of lies? I want to fast-forward time, to get out of this house, to go down to the police station in the morning away from Mrs. Maxwell and the memory of Phillipa's accident. I'll tell them everything, about the note Phillipa slipped me, about the scarves I gifted her, the ones Mrs. Maxwell insists she stole.

But in the meantime ...

I think about my conversation with Gus. When I called him, I expected him to laugh away my worries about Beatrice being involved in Phillipa's death. Instead, he sounded even more convinced than I was that I'm in the middle of something both criminal and dangerous. And what if he's right? What if Mrs. Maxwell tripped Phillipa or threw her down the stairs to silence her, so she couldn't tell me everything she knows?

Everything she knew, that is.

Maybe I should sign the piece of paper, lock myself safely back in the Maxwell guest room, then tomorrow I'll tell the police what really happened. I don't think they can get me in trouble for signing a false statement if I explain I was under duress, right? But what constitutes duress? Yes, I'm exhausted and sleep deprived and definitely not in my right mind.

On the other hand, it's not like Mrs. Maxwell is holding a gun to my head and forcing a pen into my hand.

I wish I was the type of person who could stand up to women like Mrs. Maxwell. "You know, Beatrice," I'd say, my voice full of confidence and self-respect, "I've thought about what's on this page, and the truth is I don't feel right about signing a statement that I didn't write, especially when I'm too tired to give it my full attention. Tomorrow, I plan to go to the police station and tell them everything myself. I want to thank you for offering your attorney and trying to take some of the weight of this responsibility off my hands, but I won't be signing this form."

The words sound so simple, and yet I know I don't have the strength to ever speak them. If I tried, they'd come out like a squeak, and I'd choke on them the moment Mrs. Maxwell raised an eyebrow or offered me a sideways glance of disapproval. I wish James was here. He'd take my side, explain to his mom that there's no need for me to sign this paper now since the police will want to talk to me in just a few hours anyway. She'd listen to him. She'd have to.

Unless James is somehow caught up in this entire mess as well. I glance at my phone. Where is he?

My thoughts are interrupted when Beatrice comes back into the room holding a tray with two jumbo mugs. "Here we are," she says with a smile, setting the tray down and handing me my cup.

"Drink up, and then once we're both more awake and alert, we can discuss this unsettling predicament."

# CHAPTER 29

THE CONCOCTION I'M DRINKING is far too strong and terribly bitter. Beatrice doesn't seem to realize that one of my only true vices is adding far too much sugar to my coffee. But right now, I need the caffeine and mental clarity, not the taste, so I force myself to sip down the awful black sludge.

Beatrice's voice remains saccharine as she reads me the page that her attorney has typed up, but the sound of her droning on and on combined with my tiredness and the convoluted legal jargon is lulling me into a heavy fog. I can't tell if I'm dizzy or if my body is actually gyrating while I sit, and I worry that if I were to stand up, my legs wouldn't support my weight.

"Daphne?" Beatrice pauses and sets down her paper. She sounds concerned. "Are you feeling all right?"

I try to answer her, but my tongue gets jumbled in my mouth.

"Here, let me help you onto the deck and get you some fresh air." She takes my arm and leads me outside, supporting the majority of my weight as I shuffle along on my feet.

The summer sky is bright, but it's hours before downtown Anchorage starts to wake up to start the day. There's a coastal breeze that helps me feel a bit more alert but does nothing to alleviate the onset of nausea. I lean over the railing for just a moment before I realize that if I were to throw up this bitter coffee it'd end up in the Maxwells' jacuzzi beneath us, so instead I take a deep breath, try to calm my nerves, and pray for strength.

"You've had a terrible night." Beatrice hasn't let go of my arm. "First that awful bombshell about your relationship." She shakes her head, and watching the movement makes me even dizzier. Mrs. Maxwell pulls out a deck chair and I collapse into it. "It's terrible what James did to you, really. Secretly dating the hired help, and all while he's engaged to be married to you."

I feel like Beatrice's words should elicit some type of response, but my body and brain have lost the ability to communicate with each other.

Mrs. Maxwell sighs dramatically. "I guess I'll have to tell the police that when you found out James was cheating on you with my maid, you just lost it. I didn't want to tell them everything last night when it happened. It was just so vulgar and embarrassing, but then I slept on it and realized I had to come clean and disclose the whole truth. Tell them how I heard you and Phillipa fighting about James, how you'd discovered this affair they'd been carrying on behind your back. I came out of my room to see what was the matter, right in time to watch you push Phillipa to her death. In fact, it's a more compelling story than the one we've got here."

Beatrice waves her attorney's paper in my face, then turns to the gas grill on the deck. There's a small clicking sound as the burner ignites, and she touches the page to the fire, grinning as it flames up then disintegrates to ash.

"There now, let me see if I've got the story straight. James was dating Phillipa, and you found out. You confronted her, but she denied it. There was screaming and yelling, and by the time I got out of my room to break the two of you up, you had pushed Phillipa down the stairs, whoops, just like that."

Mrs. Maxwell is getting more and more animated as she speaks. I'm certain I'm supposed to be doing something, but I can't for the life of me figure out what. Her words are mesmerizing, enchanting, and as much as I long to close my eyes and let sleep carry me away to oblivion, I can't stop listening to her.

"I didn't tell the officers everything, not right at first," she continues. "I was worried. I wanted to protect you. I always felt somewhat motherly towards you, you see. But then I got news that Phillipa died and realized if I didn't tell the police the full truth, I was just as good as an accomplice to murder. As for you, Daphne, well you'd never meant to kill the poor thing, and you were distraught over learning about James' deceit. I didn't hear a sound last night. I took one of my sleeping pills to calm me down after all that happened. It's perfectly understandable. But when I woke up in the morning, there you were floating in the hot tub. You must have flung yourself off the deck, and of course when they investigate they'll see you were in quite an impaired state to begin with, after ODing on the sleeping pills you stole from my room."

Finally, as if a coastal wind has blown away some of the heaviness in my brain, danger warnings zing through my entire body.

"That's not what happened." I'm confident I speak the words, but they make no sense to my ears when I hear them come out.

Beatrice just chuckles. "Poor thing. When they perform the autopsy they'll find all those sleeping pills in your system. You were in such bad shape you must have snuck into my medicine cabinet without me hearing you and taken the whole bottle before you jumped off the deck and fell to your death."

Beatrice has grabbed my arm, forcing me to my feet as if I were no heavier than James's dog. Thoughts of Jasper make me wonder if he'll notice once I stop coming by every day. A glimpse of the parsonage pops into my mind, that cozy home I've already started mentally preparing for James and me. I can't let this woman take that future away from us. I raise my arm, but my limbs are operating mindlessly, and instead of hitting Mrs. Maxwell, I simply flail about. For a second, I lose my balance, nearly toppling myself over the deck railing and making Beatrice's job that much easier.

I think about my mother. If something were to happen to me, she'd spend the rest of her life alone in Pioneer Peaks, seeing nobody but the nurses and orderlies day in and day out. I know Gus would take care of her, but he's just one person. I won't abandon her. Not again.

The thought gives me a surge of physical strength and mental clarity.

"Let me go." The words don't come out correctly, but I don't care. I tug myself out of Beatrice's grasp. She lunges after me. We fall to the deck floor. I have no plan but to defend myself. I have no intentions of dying today, of leaving my mother entirely alone.

I kick and flail, desperate to protect myself. I'm nauseated, sleep-deprived, and drugged, but I'm going to do whatever it takes to survive.

So help me God, this is not how my life is going to end.

# CHAPTER 30

"PHILLIPA WAS SO MUCH easier to kill," Beatrice grunts.

I have no idea if I'm hallucinating these words or not. It's possible I'm fighting back as Beatrice tries to strangle me. It's possible I'm doing absolutely nothing, just waiting here, frozen in fear, feeling the pain but not nearly as acutely as I might have expected.

Then again, perhaps none of this is happening at all. Perhaps I'm already unconscious.

Or perhaps I'm entirely crazy like my father, imagining everything.

If I had to guess, I think I'm still struggling, still desperate to survive, but I can't be sure it isn't all in my head. Are those my hands swatting at my assailant, or is that just what my brain is trying to tell me to do?

For some strange reason, a memory flashes through my mind, a documentary Mom and I watched together years ago. A hiker finds himself stranded in a storm on Mount Everest. He manages to radio the others at base camp, and for two hours they talk him through the treacherous trek back to safety. As he makes his way back to them, he describes the landmarks he passes, receives step-by-step descriptions from his team telling him exactly where to go, where to turn, how to get back. His voice sounds more and more hopeful as he gets closer to camp, but it turns out it was all in his mind.

In reality, his body had stopped moving entirely, and his brain was making up the entire descent.

He died on top of the mountain in that snowstorm, in the exact location where he first got stranded.

Mom was so upset. She felt so sorry for the deceased hiker and the mourning family and friends he left behind.

A woman's hands are around my throat. I picture myself grabbing her fingers to loosen their hold around my neck, but I don't think my appendages are actually moving at all.

As my vision starts to fade, a distant song floats on the coastal breeze, faint enough that I can just barely make out the familiar melody.

*Amazing grace, how sweet the sound ...*

The words are calming, like a lullaby, and I realize that maybe I don't need to fight so hard after all. I'm so very tired, and the haunting refrain is so comforting.

*That saved a wretch like me.*

I'm no longer struggling, not physically or mentally. Instead, I'm straining to hear the heavenly music that washes over me like a healing bath. I'm intellectually aware that my body hurts, but this knowledge doesn't seem to impact me whatsoever, like viewing a scary movie and realizing that none of what you're watching is real.

*I once was lost, but now I'm found ...*

My eyes have shut, but instead of black and nothingness, I see lights, crystal clear and shining, water shimmering on a pristine lake. I feel my body spasm and panic as it tries in vain to suck in air, but even though I'm flailing in a desperate search for oxygen, it's like it's happening to another person entirely.

*Was blind, but now I see.*

"Get your hands off of her, now."

A body slams into my attacker, and at the same instant breath rushes into my lungs. I struggle to sit up and cough, but I'm so very weak.

"What are you doing?"

The voice brings a flood of joy and relief, almost as welcomed as the air that I suck in greedily.

James. James is here. My fiancé has come to rescue me. He pulls his mother off me.

"She attacked me!" Mrs. Maxwell spits. "She came out here going on like mad accusing me of pushing Phillipa down the stairs. I denied it, of course, and she just turned feral."

James steps between his mother and the spot where I sit on the floor. "Get away from my fiancé," he orders with a menacing growl in his voice.

Tears sting my eyes. I'm so happy to hear him. I'm so happy to breathe.

"This woman has ruined everything in your life," Mrs. Maxwell hisses at him.

James snorts disdainfully. "Strong words from the woman who knocked me out with chloroform and locked me in the attic."

"I did that to protect you. Trust me, you have no idea what damage this strumpet is going to cause all of us. She's going to ruin everything."

For a moment, I'm certain James is going to hit his mother. "You're the one who ruined everything when you started colluding with Senator Danvers," he shouts.

"Ha, you see!" She turns to me triumphantly. "It's all about Danvers, you heard it yourself. Trust me, my son has never loved you. He's never gotten over Manderley. He adores her. He worships her. You're just the distraction, a means to an end. That's why I had to kill your father, to keep him from spreading his terrible lies about our family."

James has helped me to my feet, still keeping his body between Beatrice and me, but I'm too weak to stand and sink into one of the chairs. He reaches into his pocket. "Where did you put my phone? I'm calling the police."

Beatrice clutches her son by the arm. "James, forget all this. Forget her, forget what you saw. Let me finish what I need to do. Trust me when I tell you this is all for the best. I'll take the fall for it. You can tell the police you didn't get here in time. You can blame it all on me. But we can't leave her as a witness or she is going to destroy everything. Everything," she repeats and a bit of spittle lands on my lap.

I'm still struggling to overcome my nausea and thirst for oxygen. I want James to ignore his mother, to come to me and take me far away from here. But he doesn't move.

"You can have Manderley, darling." Beatrice's voice is desperate and grating. "Manderley is the love of your life, your soulmate. You know that as well as I do. It's time you learned the truth. We needed Daphne to sign that paper so she wouldn't tell anyone about her father or what she's learned about our business. And now it's signed. It's done. It's time for you and Manderley to settle down like you always dreamed of. The two of you can be so happy together. We just need to make sure that this one pathetic mistake doesn't spoil it all."

James and his mother stare at each other, and for the briefest second I wonder if her words have enchanted him, if he'll leave me to suffer whatever fate Beatrice has planned for me and go and live out his happily ever after with the senator's daughter.

I hold my breath, suspended. It's as if God has pressed the pause button until the entire world stops moving.

Then James shakes his head like his dog would shake away a mosquito. "You're crazy."

He turns toward me, but before I can utter a warning, Mrs. Maxwell rushes toward him, swinging a deck chair over her head and bringing it down on his back. He falls forward. Mrs. Maxwell grabs me by my arms and shoves until my head hangs over the deck railing.

"Mom, no!" I hear James shout.

For a moment I'm flying, straining my ears to hear that trace of heavenly music.

Then a crack interrupts my fall, and I'm surrounded by pain and blackness and nothing.

# CHAPTER 31

"Hey, look. It's Sleeping Beauty. About time you woke up."

I blink, wondering why the light is so bright overhead. I try to raise my hand to shield my eyes and panic when I realize there's gauze and tubes covering nearly every part of my visible body.

"No sudden movements or anything," a familiar voice tells me. "You've had two surgeries already and there's a tube sticking out of your chest, but the nurses seem to think it'll get removed soon. Just take it easy."

Her face comes into focus, and I'm relieved when I recognize her. "Becca?" I try to speak, but my vocal cords don't form any words. There's something wrong with my face, but I have no idea what it is.

"The nurse said you might be disoriented and that's totally normal. Can you hear me? Give me a blink if you can."

*Blink.*

My roommate smiles at me. "Good. I've already pushed the call button, so I'm sure the nurses will be in here soon fussing over you. I can't believe my best friend has turned into such a local celebrity. Do you hurt anywhere? Give me a blink if you're okay."

Okay? How should I know? But Becca looks so worried, and I want to alleviate her fears.

*Blink.*

Another smile, and she reaches out and touches my fingers. "Okay. Welcome back to the land of the living. I don't want to sound overly dramatic, but at first we didn't know if you were going to make it. Well, the doctors weren't sure. I told them all you were tough, and I knew you'd want to get better so you can marry that trust-fund pastor of yours."

Something in her words is distasteful, but I can't pinpoint exactly what it is. I'm still tired.

So very tired.

I sense movement around me, other voices in my ears, other faces in my field of vision. All I want to do is disappear into nothing.

A little more sleep couldn't hurt.

# CHAPTER 32

FOUR DAYS AFTER I first awaken, I can sit up in my hospital bed, relatively tube free. In addition to multiple bone fractures in my ribs and the side of my face, I've got a punctured lung and broken collar bone. I'm bruised and bandaged and pumped up with pain meds, but my mind feels relatively clear as Becca and I thumb through a new bridal magazine.

"At least now with James's mother in jail you can plan the wedding exactly how you want," she tells me. "No meddling mother-in-law-zilla to interfere or anything." Becca lets out a small chuckle then looks at me playfully. "Come on. You know I'm just teasing you."

"I know." Maybe one day I'll be able to laugh at the ordeal I just survived, but it won't be today, and not just because it hurts to smile with a shattered cheekbone.

"Too soon?" Becca asks.

"Yeah."

"Okay." She thumbs open to a full-page spread she's bookmarked. "Well, on another note, I was thinking that if you decided to go with the baby blue color scheme, this type of bridesmaid dress would be amazing, am I right?" She holds the page up toward her face. "See? It totally brings out my eyes."

Becca has been in every day, keeping me company, sharing the diner gossip she loves to spread, showing me funny wedding fail videos she thinks will make me laugh. When there's a lull in the conversation she likes to bring up plans for my big day, but I can hardly think about that at the moment.

Before I can respond, we're interrupted by a man's voice. "Special delivery." James stands in the doorway, holding a huge vase full of colorful flowers, a rainbow of tulips like the kind my mother adores.

"Guess that's my cue to leave." Becca gets up and is out of the room without another word to either of us. Even though they're both here to see me each and every day, I doubt either of them have spoken more than a dozen words to each other since I first woke up after the accident.

Becca's my best friend and maid of honor, but she and James hardly know each other. Becca usually works at the diner on Sundays when we go to church, and there's no reason for James to hang out at our apartment when the parsonage is so cozy and convenient. For a second, I think about Jasper and wonder if the sweet dog misses me or if he'll be scared when he sees me looking so changed after they let me out of here, if he'll smell my internal injuries and know that something's wrong with me.

James takes a step toward my bed. "Hiya."

I do my best to smile, even though my cheek and face and head and entire body ache. "Hey."

James doesn't move. Part of me wants him to lean over and kiss me like he used to. Part of me wants to fast-forward to whatever point in time means that neither of us feels guilty or scared or somehow ashamed when we're together.

James looks about as uncomfortable as I feel, so I force myself to say something. "Those are pretty flowers."

"Oh, these?" He looks down in surprise, as if he'd forgotten he was holding them. "Yeah, they're not from me. They're from Mrs. van Hopper and the ladies in her Bible study group. She brought them to church, and there's a card they all signed too."

The thought of Mrs. van Hopper brings a genuine sense of warm gratitude. When I needed reconstructive surgery after my cheekbone was completely shattered in the fall, her husband recommended the very best in the state and got me on his schedule as an emergency addition.

"Your bruises are looking better today," James says as he sets the flowers on the window sill. "How are you feeling?"

"Still weaning off the pain meds now, so that's good."

"That's good," James repeats. He doesn't seem to know if he should sit or stand, come closer or walk away. I wish I could tell him which I preferred, but I'm just as lost as he is.

"You know I hate myself for what happened to you." He's staring at my pillow, not at my face, as if the sight of me is actually too hideous for him to bear.

"It's not your fault. I'm just glad you showed up when you did."

"Don't thank me," he says, still not meeting my gaze. "We both know who the real hero of the night was."

For a moment, we're silent. I think about Gus's role in my rescue. Sensing I was in danger, he never ended our phone call, so he was on the line the entire time I was struggling with Mrs. Maxwell. He heard everything, called 911 from his landline, and put the call on speaker. That's why the police were there in time to pull me out of the hot tub before I drowned, and how they got all the evidence they needed to arrest Beatrice Maxwell for killing Phillipa and attempting to do the same to me.

James and I stare at the vase of flowers, and I long for the days when conversations between the two of us were so easy and natural. There was a time when I assumed that nothing could come between the two of us, that the love we shared was designed and sanctioned by God himself and therefore invincible.

Unbreakable.

It's hard to explain exactly what happened. Hard to guess where we'll go from here. It's clear now that James' mother acted alone when she set us up at the diner, and it's obvious that the only reason she did so was to get me to sign a prenup agreeing to never speak about my dad. At the time, she had no idea Phillipa knew as much as she did or that she'd talk with a private investigator, which is why she pushed her down the stairs to silence her testimony forever.

So now, James and I are here, in a hospital room where I'm recovering from attempted murder. I'm never going to be the same person I was a week ago, before Mrs. Maxwell got her hands on me. Even if the physical wounds all heal, the scars will remain forever.

I think James knows this. And he's changed too. Which maybe explains why every time he comes to visit me here, I feel like we're in a drawn-out process of saying goodbye.

We've never talked about it, not directly. I need to focus on my healing and recovery, and James is too compassionate to throw something like this on me right now. But just like I know that soon the days will shorten, the sun will eventually set, and autumn will come and bring with it the assurance of winter, I know that once I'm past the most intense stage of my recovery, there are questions that James and I will need to face. Hard questions. Seemingly impossible questions.

Like how do you move on if you know that your entire relationship was built on a lie, even if it was a lie neither of you were aware of at the time?

And how do you learn to trust anyone ever again after seeing the worst depravity that humanity can display?

Each and every time James looks at me, he sees the wounds his own mother inflicted. And the bitterness is a poison that might consume him entirely.

When I look at him, I see the child of the woman who tried to murder me. I'm not sure any amount of prayer or therapy will completely take away the fear I feel at the core of my soul.

Is even the strongest love able to completely overcome all this? Ten years from now, if James sees the scar on my jaw, will he still look as broken and devastated as he does today? If I'm carrying James' baby and my mended rib fractures again, will I blame my husband for the pain I'm forced to endure?

There are other obstacles too, obstacles I'm not ready to admit out loud. Because when James talked to me about Manderley Danvers, I saw the pain and hurt and despair their breakup caused him.

And when his mother said he still adored her — regardless of the fact that Mrs. Maxwell is a vengeful, murderous criminal who's going to spend the rest of her life in prison — I think there's a tiny part of me that knew she spoke the truth.

# CHAPTER 33

*Three months later*

The sun is starting to rise when Becca waves goodbye and heads out the door to start her shift at the diner. I'm working the lunch hour today. Danny's been great about letting me come back on a part-time basis so I can continue all my physical therapy and regular visits with my mom. An autumn chill is in the air, and a school bus rolls by noisily outside.

I grab my cup of coffee, add about a quarter cup of pumpkin spice creamer, and spread out my journal and art supplies. Today's the day I need to make my decision about James, and I still don't know what I'm going to choose. James and I have been meeting with a couples counselor, a woman named Cheryl who's helping us unpack everything that happened last summer. Beatrice Maxwell remains in jail, no chance of bail, and it seems as if every week the papers are discovering more and more of her scandals as prosecutors prepare for her trial. Mr. Maxwell will almost certainly be indicted as well, and he's been getting his affairs in order and has no contact with any of his kids.

James has resigned from his position at the church. Even though he had nothing to do with his parents' shady business dealings, he wasn't willing to let the Maxwell scandal impact Anchorage Grace. They're kind enough to let him stay at the parsonage until he figures out what his next step will be, and a big part of that decision is based on whatever I'm going to tell our counselor this afternoon.

If ever there was a day for prayer, this is it.

I flip to Proverbs, which seems like a smart place to start since I'm asking God for guidance and wisdom.

*Do not forsake wisdom, and she will protect you; love her, and she will watch over you.* Instantly I think about my mother, her gentle hands working their way through my hair. She's moved into a better care facility, thanks to the trust the Maxwells set up. I had no idea I was doing so at the time, but when I signed that prenup and accepted the trust fund for my mother's care, I was actually giving the Maxwells total control over my mother's health decisions. That means if at any point I dared to go against their wishes or expose any corruption I discovered, they could pull my mom out of whatever home she was in or deny her care entirely. Their goal was to turn my mother into a complete hostage, knowing I'd do anything to guarantee her wellbeing. Thankfully, James and I have already hired two separate lawyers. We've signed dozens of forms to ensure the prenup is completely null and void, but the very real trust his parents set up for my mom has been transferred to my management.

*A friend loves at all times, and a brother is born for a time of adversity.* The best news is that Gus has transitioned with my mom to the better facility, and he is now her primary caregiver five days a week. It's a better schedule for him, more consistency for my mother, and I couldn't be more thankful for how that side of this ordeal all worked out in the end.

*For through wisdom your days will be many, and years will be added to your life.* The medical director at Mom's new home got her on a new experimental drug. We're still working on getting the dosage exactly right, but I'm thrilled that she's singing regularly again. Gus sends me videos nearly every day. He wants to start a YouTube channel, but I've had enough publicity to last me my entire life, and I think Mom would prefer to keep her music private as well.

Besides, as I like to remind Gus, Mom's repertoire at the moment consists of only one hymn, in spite of how fervently and faithfully she sings it.

*A cheerful heart is good medicine.* My recovery comes in bits and spurts. I'm off all the prescription meds, but my shoulder aches as the days grow colder, and I can't chew tough foods anymore without aggravating my jaw.

Becca and I have grown even closer. Now that I'm back home from the hospital, we spend nearly every evening watching funny sitcoms on TV, enough to make me laugh, to remind me that the world can still be full of joy.

My pen is poised over the page, but when I think about the question my counselor asked me last week, I'm no closer to a response.

When I came home from the hospital, James and I both thought it was best to take everything slow. We needed to reassess each step of our relationship with the hindsight of how it all began and how our families are connected by tragedy, crime, and scandal. Our counselor, Cheryl, is a gift from God, and she's the one who encouraged us to resist the urge to come up with a label to redefine our relationship too quickly. We're not exactly engaged, but we haven't broken up. We haven't erased the tentative wedding plans on our calendar for next fall, but we aren't actively planning the ceremony either. When we're together, there's plenty of love between us in spite of the somewhat pained awkwardness that persists, but we're seeing less and less of each other, like two separate ice floes being carried off by two opposing currents.

For a season, this limbo state made sense. My brain was foggy coming off my meds, and we were both reeling from everything that happened — certainly not the right mental framework for making life-changing decisions. But now that James has resigned from the church, we need to come to a more formal agreement about our future. Eventually James will move out of the parsonage, and we still aren't sure if he should be looking for a place for him or a place for us.

If the future includes an us, he might even look for a home that's accessible to my mother and hire round-the-clock care so we can all live together.

If the future doesn't include an us, he really has no reason to stay in Alaska at all, what with its tainted memories and his family's tarnished reputation.

And so I'm here, sitting at my folding table, flipping through Proverbs, scribbling down the verses that catch my eye. In a way, I'm surprised to find myself in such a dilemma, because on the surface Cheryl's question sounds very simple: *If I met James for the first time today, is he the man I'd fall in love with and want to marry?*

Cheryl asked him a similar question. He met with her yesterday, but I don't know what response he gave. He and I weren't supposed to talk about it. Not yet.

Today after my shift at the diner, I'll go and meet with Cheryl by myself. Tonight, she'll go home with the information we've both given her, and tomorrow we'll all meet together to discuss the future.

I love James. I love his kind heart, his integrity that somehow stayed intact in spite of his family's greed and corruption.

I love the way he came to my rescue that terrifying night and the memories we built together before the summer ripped our hearts to shreds.

I love James. But is he the man I'd fall in love with today if I met him for the first time?

My pen hasn't moved, and my coffee's turned cold. I pull out my cell phone.

There's someone I need to talk to.

"Good morning, sunshine." The voice on the other end of the line is cheerful and calming, like I knew it would be.

"Hey, there," I answer back. "Just wanted to say hi. And to thank you for taking such good care of my mom."

Gus lets out a joyful chuckle. "I should be the one thanking you for getting me this cushy position. Besides, you know how much I love your mom. She's my favorite patient by far, but don't tell the others I said that, okay?"

"I promise." Talking with Gus has become a bright spot in each and every one of my days. Sometimes it's just a quick call to hear how Mom's doing. Sometimes we'll chat about hardly anything at all, like we do now on Gus's morning commute. Hearing his voice makes me feel less alone, less uncertain. We don't talk about James or about my upcoming therapy appointment with Cheryl, but I already feel so much better.

"Hey," he eventually announces, "I just pulled in. Let me put you on mute, then after I clock in you can say hi to your mom."

"Sounds good." I sit looking at my phone and sipping at my coffee, which has turned lukewarm. A quiet has settled over my soul. A few leaves shake in the wind outside my apartment window and float on the breeze in a graceful dance. The sun shines vividly, and it feels as if all of nature has decided to worship God this fall morning by creating something pure. Something inspiring.

Something beautiful.

"Daphne, you there?" Gus asks, and his voice brings a smile to my already overflowing heart. "Okay," he says, "I'm putting you on speaker. Good morning, pretty lady. Did you have a good sleep, Mrs. Winters?"

"Oh." Mom's voice sounds strong and happy on the other end of the line. "You came."

"Yup, it's me." In my mind, I can picture the way Gus walks over to her bed and picks up her hand in his, so calmly and naturally, like I've seen him do dozens of times. "How are you, Mrs. Winters?"

"Oh, I think I'm pretty good."

"You think, huh?" His voice resonates with laughter and compassion and delight, and again I thank God for bringing such a perfect caretaker into our lives.

"I have a surprise for you this morning," Gus says. I love the way he speaks to Mom clearly and loudly but without infantilizing her in the process.

"A surprise?" I can hear the smile in my mom's voice.

"Yup, there's someone on the phone who wants to say good morning. Want to guess who it is?" Gus asks playfully.

"Who is it?"

"It's Daphne."

There's silence on the other end, and I temper my expectations. Some days Mom gets confused by the phone and doesn't know who she's talking to. Some days even when I'm standing in front of her she has no idea who I am.

"Daphne." Mom breathes the word out softly, like the gentle autumn wind. "Daphne." There's a light now in her voice, a spark of recognition, and I can hear her take a deep breath. "Oh, Daphne. You know, she's the greatest thing that's ever happened to me, that sweet little girl of mine."

"I bet she is," Gus responds. "Well, you say good morning to Daphne, and then I'm going to help you make your way to the ladies' room, okay?"

I talk to Mom for a couple minutes, even though the cell phone confuses her and I don't think she understands who I am or where my voice is coming from. Gus asks me what time I'll be coming by to visit today and says he'll try to plan his work break accordingly. After we say goodbye, I sit and continue to stare at my journal, at all these verses from Proverbs I've written down.

Soon I'll have to make up my mind about James, but right now I simply rest in this peace that's washed over me after talking to my mom.

Outside, a squirrel runs across a power line. He stops for a moment outside my window and stares at me curiously, like I'm the first human he's ever seen. Then, as quick as he arrived, he's gone. I wonder if somewhere in there is a message from God, a sign about what I'm supposed to tell Cheryl when we meet today.

I've built so many beautiful images in my mind of a future with James. Living together at the Anchorage Grace parsonage or somewhere just as cozy. Playing with the dog every night, taking long hikes with James and Jasper on the weekends.

There are so many things about our future I can see so clearly.

But Cheryl's question still unsettles me. *If I met James for the first time today, is he the man I'd fall in love with and want to marry?*

The answer should be easy, but it's not.

The sound of my mother singing pulls me out of my thoughts. *Amazing grace, how sweet the sound that saved a wretch like me.*

In the background, I hear Gus's muffled voice telling her how much he loves to hear her sing. It's the second time this year that Gus didn't end our phone call when I thought he had. Last summer, it ended up saving my life.

This morning, it has done the same.

Because as I sit here listening to my mother sing, as I bask in the bright fall sunlight and soak in every ounce of love and peace and blessing that God is pouring out on my thirsty soul, I have my answer.

*I once was lost, but now I'm found.*

I know what future God has planned for me, and it's glorious and it's beautiful and it's better than anything I could have dared dream possible.

*Was blind but now I see.*

# CHAPTER 34

*Thirteen Months Later*

"I adore fall weddings," Becca gushes as she zips me into my dress and sighs dreamily. "The only thing I love more are spring weddings. And summer weddings," she adds and adjusts a curl in my hair.

She looks out the window of the church, where the leaves on the trees have turned orange.

"It'll be winter soon," she muses.

I fidget with the clasp of my necklace. "Yeah, James said we might get snow as early as next weekend."

"Well, good thing the ceremony isn't any later. Although I do love winter weddings. Here, do you want me to buckle that for you?" She takes the necklace and fastens it in place on the first try.

"Thanks," I tell her, and for a moment I remember a time when I had perfect mobility in my shoulders and could put on any piece of jewelry with ease. But I've promised not to let any maudlin thoughts damper the joy of today, and I quickly change the subject. "You don't think the necklace is too out of place with this dress?"

Becca tilts her head to the side, staring at my reflection in the mirror. "No, I mean, everybody who knows you understands how special it is to you."

I finger the white gold heart around my neck, a present Gus gave me last Christmas after Mom died. A small dove is etched on one side, a reminder of her calm and peaceful passing, how she simply stopped breathing and her soul was released to heaven.

On the back side two words are engraved.

*Amazing Grace.*

"She would be so happy for you," Becca says quietly, running her fingers gently over my curls.

There's a knock at the door. "We're about to start."

Becca's cousin is our wedding planner, and I've enjoyed the interactions we've had immensely. Now that James is working for a non-profit program for refugee children, a celebrity planner like Elle wouldn't have exactly fit the budget anyway. James has enough in trusts to not have to worry much about finances, but because of his parents' very public scandal, he takes a lot of pains to never appear flashy. A lot of his money is going directly to charity, and he's also helping Phillipa's family cover their legal expenses in their wrongful death lawsuit against his mother.

I think it's his way of trying to atone for his parents' crimes.

Becca gives me a quick kiss on the top of my head in a gesture that's surprisingly gentle. "I'll see you at the reception," she says. "Save me a spot!" She laughs, apparently still completely scandalized at the idea of a wedding reception without assigned seats.

I check the clasp of my necklace once more, then I follow the wedding planner to the sanctuary.

I've never loved being the center of attention, and I feel my face heating up as I make that slow, awkward procession down the aisle. James is standing by the pulpit, the same pulpit he preached behind when he served as the pastor here, and we smile at each other.

I take my place on the opposite side of the stage, turn around, and wait.

The traditional wedding march has been replaced with something quiet and unobtrusive, much like the bride herself as she appears in the sanctuary doorway. Manderley is wearing a plain-cut white gown. It's a similar style to my lavender bridesmaid dress, the only difference being that hers carries the hint of a train behind her.

Her silky black hair cascades in gentle waves around her face, which beams as she stares adoringly at her groom.

I think back over everything that's happened in the past year and a half, all the twists and turns that have brought each of us to where we are today. James, about to marry his true soulmate. And me, on the stage as one of Manderley's bridesmaids, thankful to have her in my life as a friend.

Some people were surprised that she asked me to stand with her at her wedding, given my previous relationship with the groom, but there's a peace that settles on my soul today, and I'm convinced this was God's plan for each one of us from the very beginning.

I look out into the faces in the congregation. In the middle section, I see Becca, who smiles, and Gus, who catches my eye and winks. With a full and overflowing heart, I thank the Lord for these people he's brought into my life, thankful for their love and compassion and support they show me day after day.

"Dearly beloved." Anchorage Grace's new pastor begins his oration, a combination of both traditional and contemporary elements. Outside a gentle breeze rustles in the trees, and I watch through the sanctuary window as a solitary orange leaf cascades gracefully down toward the ground.

# CHAPTER 35

"OH, DAPHNE, IT'S SO lovely to see you." Mrs. van Hopper makes her way immediately from the buffet line to my table in the reception hall. She leans down and gives me a hug. "You look beautiful, darling," she declares, twice as loudly as necessary. "Nobody would ever believe you've had face work done, either. Oh, is this seat taken? I just want to pop down for a minute. It's been forever since we've talked. You're doing well, I assume?"

Now that I've gotten to know her better, I'm amused at how I used to be simultaneously annoyed and intimidated by this woman, who turns out to be nothing but a kindly matron with a voice that carries too far.

"It was a beautiful ceremony, wasn't it?" Mrs. van Hopper pops a deviled egg into her mouth. "Just perfect. I'm so glad you stood up there with them. I think that really made their day so special. And what a lovely couple they are, aren't they?"

I smile and have to agree.

"I just love how you and Manderley became so close after everything you all went through. Speaking of, I hear they still haven't set a date for the Maxwell trial?"

I shrug. Until I'm compelled to testify about Mrs. Maxwell's vicious attack, I don't want to have anything to do with James' parents or their legal drama.

"Well then," Mrs. van Hopper continues, "it really is just a beautiful example of Romans 8, isn't it? God works all things together for good. James and Manderley, you and your dashing man. Where is that handsome hubby of yours anyway?"

"Right behind you, Mrs. Van Hopper."

"Oh, dear!" Mrs. Van Hopper's look of surprise makes this already joyful occasion even more hilarious. Gus and I both laugh as she scoots over one chair so he can sit next to me.

"I know better than to come between two young newlyweds like both of you," she declares with a wink. "Scarcely back from your honeymoon, and now here celebrating another wedding."

"It's definitely been a busy year," Gus agrees. He leans over and kisses my cheek. "You look so beautiful today, sweetie."

I lean my head against his chest and adjust my wedding band, wondering if I'll ever get so accustomed to wearing it that it ceases to fill me with awe and gratitude every time I twist it around my finger.

If that day ever does come, I know it won't be any time soon.

A few minutes later, Becca joins our table. "I still liked your wedding better," she whispers to me.

I chuckle. "That's because I put you in charge of every single detail so you could make it exactly how you wanted."

Becca ignores my joke. "Hey, Gus," she says, nudging him in the ribs. "How many old-people diapers you end up changing this week?"

"I'd tell you, but I don't want you to have to take off your shoes to count that high," he teases back playfully.

After everyone has made their way through the buffet line, the pastor sets up the microphone for anybody who wants to make a toast.

"You gonna say anything?" Becca asks me in a whisper.

"No." I thought about it, but everything I wanted to tell both James and Manderley is in the card I included with their wedding present, a painting I made for them based on a verse from Song of Solomon.

*I am my beloved's, and my beloved is mine.*

While a few of their friends stand up and wish them love and joy and blessings in their marriage, I hold Gus's hand, so thankful to have this man by my side.

The wedding song Manderley and James chose for their first dance is *God Bless the Broken Road*, and I almost cry when I think about all the ways God has worked in my life and the lives of my friends, bringing the right people together at exactly the right time, in spite of how hard the road was to get us all to where we are today.

When the next song begins, others are invited to join the bride and groom. Gus holds out his hand to me, and I take his in mine.

"May I have this dance?" His smile radiates love and tenderness and everything I adore about my husband.

I smile as he leads me to the dance floor.

"I thought you'd never ask."

# FROM THE AUTHOR

I HOPE YOU ENJOYED reading Daphne's journey in *Toils and Snares*. Did you catch the hidden secret behind the names of most of the characters?

This is the very first full-length novel I wrote, edited, *and* published after taking time off the creative work of writing due to stress, pandemic, and life. It felt so good to be back to work again ... and also a little scary!

I'm so thankful to my prayer partner Jaime who let me borrow some of her mother's story to show me what it's like to have a parent with dementia. Also to Laura who drove me out of the way just hours after we met so I could get a cord for my laptop while traveling in Juneau. And a big hello to my business partner Julie, who primarily writes romance and doesn't like things too violent and finally has a novel of mine she can read!

I've called Alaska home for the vast majority of my adult life, and I love writing about its untamed beauty, terrifying wilderness, and sometimes baffling politics. (As an aside, we probably have the largest number of politicians who have died in mysterious plane crashes out of any state!)

If you're craving more fast-paced, Alaska-based Christian suspense, full of danger, excitement, and a touch of romance, you can dive straight into the *Alaskan Refuge* series. This collection of three Christian mysteries delves deeper into the heart of Alaska's wilderness, where faith is tested and trust becomes a matter of survival. Each book promises edge-of-your-seat thrills set against the stunning backdrop of this extraordinary state.

You can shop our Alaska Christian fiction sale at sale.christianbooks.today/alaska-refuge... Just be prepared to stay up late!

Printed in the USA
CPSIA information can be obtained
at www.ICGtesting.com
JSHW022227161124
73601JS00003B/13